Cowboy at Heart

SHIPMENT FIVE

Belonging to Bandera by Tina Leonard
Court Me, Cowboy by Barbara White Daille
His Best Friend's Bride by Jodi O'Donnell
The Cowboy's Return by Linda Warren
Baby Be Mine by Victoria Pade
The Cattle Baron by Margaret Way

SHIPMENT SIX

Crockett's Seduction by Tina Leonard
Coming Home to the Cattleman by Judy Christenberry
Almost Perfect by Judy Duarte
Cowboy Dad by Cathy McDavid
Real Cowboys by Roz Denny Fox
The Rancher Wore Suits by Rita Herron
Falling for the Texas Tycoon by Karen Rose Smith

SHIPMENT SEVEN

Last's Temptation by Tina Leonard
Daddy by Choice by Marin Thomas
The Cowboy, the Baby and the Bride-to-Be by Cara Colter
Luke's Proposal by Lois Faye Dyer
The Truth About Cowboys by Margot Early
The Other Side of Paradise by Laurie Paige

SHIPMENT EIGHT

Mason's Marriage by Tina Leonard
Bride at Briar's Ridge by Margaret Way
Texas Bluff by Linda Warren
Cupid and the Cowboy by Carol Finch
The Horseman's Son by Delores Fossen
Cattleman's Bride-to-Be by Lois Faye Dyer

The rugged, masculine and independent men
of America's West know the value of hard work,
honor and family. They may be ranchers, tycoons
or the guy next door, but they're all cowboys at heart.
Don't miss any of the books in this collection!

Cowboy at Heart

THE RANCHER'S PROMISE
JODI O'DONNELL

USA TODAY Bestselling Author

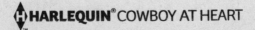

HARLEQUIN® COWBOY AT HEART

Recycling programs
for this product may
not exist in your area.

ISBN-13: 978-0-373-82624-7

THE RANCHER'S PROMISE

Copyright © 2002 by Jodi O'Donnell

Printed in U.S.A.

JODI O'DONNELL

grew up one of fourteen children in small-town
Iowa. As a result, she loves to explore in her writing
how family relationships influence who and why we
love as we do.

A *USA TODAY* bestselling author, Jodi has also
been a finalist for Romance Writers of America's
RITA® Award and is a past winner of RWA's
Golden Heart Award. She lives in Iowa.

To my Little Sis, Marie, whose friendship
has made my life so much richer.

Chapter One

Grasping the tarnished brass doorknob one more time, Lara Dearborn threw her hip into the wooden door with a burlesque bump that would have done Gypsy Rose Lee proud.

The door, no doubt warped from decades of the humidity that permeated south Texas, gave way with a jolt, sending Lara stumbling across the medical clinic's deserted waiting area. She managed to stop just short of plowing into the receiving counter opposite the entry, but in her desperate quest for balance dumped her armload of books and supplies across the scarred heart-of-pine floor. Her stethoscope, luckily protected within its case, went skidding under the sagging plaid sofa against one wall. The behemoth *Physician's Desk Reference* she carried, however, landed smack on her instep.

Lara wasn't one for using bad language, even when she was in pain. So, bending down to massage her throbbing foot, she let fly with not one, not two, but three of her favorite swearing alternatives from way back. "Shucky darn, suffering succotash and shootin' shine-ola," she exclaimed with relish, feeling much better for the effort.

The satisfying sensation lingered only a second—until a deep, masculine laugh came rumbling toward her from somewhere in the recesses of the clinic beyond the other side of the counter.

"Oh!" Lara exclaimed in surprise, and not a little embarrassment. Since it was Saturday afternoon, she'd thought she would be alone in the clinic, have some time to explore and maybe even get a little work done before she started seeing patients at the start of the week.

She had little choice but to bluster her way through this. "All right," she demanded, "who's back there?"

There was not even a second's pause. "The name's Bond." The answer came in a killer imitation of Sean Connery. "James Bond."

Then the laughter again.

Lara bent at the waist, feeling around under the sofa for her stethoscope, because once she found it—to heck with the *PDR*—she was hightailing it out that sticky front door. Not that she believed whoever it was she could hear walking toward the front of the clinic was truly dangerous. After all, this *was* Bridgewater, Texas, where everyone knew everyone else, making any stranger stand out like a sore thumb. But such a confirmation was best made in a venue where she felt a little less vulnerable.

She wasn't to be allowed even that bit of luck, either. Instead, she had just laid her hand on the black case containing her stethoscope when a cowboy stepped around the corner of the counter, saying, "May I help you, ma'am?"

At least she thought he must be a cowboy. He was dressed for the part in a pair of work-worn Wranglers, a rolled-up-at-the-sleeves, dark green Western shirt and dusty brown boots. All he lacked to complete the image was a beat-up Stetson and a lower lip stuffed with chewing tobacco.

"No. No, not at all," she said nervously, sitting back and slapping her thigh in a show of false bravado. "I—I just stopped in to, um… but now that I'm here, I'll just be, you know, getting on my way. That is, if that's all right with you, Mr., um, Mr. Bond."

Her lame attempt at dissembling brought another not entirely unattractive rumble of laughter from the man in front of her.

"Actually, the name *isn't* Bond—and I'm really not a crackpot," he said, allaying her suspicions. "It's just the way you asked who I was, not to mention that I've always wanted to say that in public, just once, instead of in front of the bathroom mirror. That and 'Go ahead—make my day.'"

At her wary look, he waved a hand dismissively. "I'm sorry," he said, although the apology was filtered through yet more laughter. "Before you stands the product of an overactive imagination. Pay no attention to me, no attention at all."

The problem was, paying no attention to him would have been impossible, even if there were a law against it. That was why she stared. He was just about as handsome as all the movie heroes he claimed to imitate in front of the bathroom mirror. Topped off with a cherry.

He had deep-set eyes the color of rich, dark chocolate, and short hair the same rich brown. His jawline could only be described as chiseled. He was tall—over six feet—with the kind of broad-shouldered, slim-hipped cowboy build that had doubtless earned him a few frankly admiring stares in his time.

But it was his smile—wide and white and just a shade wistful—that had her heart galloping as if it wanted to outrun itself. The dimples carved into both his cheeks had to be a quarter of an inch deep. At least.

The smile faded as he noticed her easing her shoe off to rub her instep.

"Are you hurt?" In a trice he was kneeling in front of her and had her ankle in his hand and her shoe the rest of the way off before she could react to being touched by a total stranger. "Lord, here I am runnin' on at the mouth, not even thinking something had set off that string of inventive cussing."

Even through her thick athletic sock, she could feel the warmth of his large hands, which, instead of making her want to jerk away, sent a definite starstruck thrill through her. Up close she got the chance to note just how thick his eyelashes were. Very. His eyebrows were dark and thick, too, and punctuated his earnest gaze in the same way his dimples did his smile.

"I'm all right, really," she said. "I'd know if I'd broken anything.... I'm the new physician's assistant here at the clinic."

He let go of her ankle, causing a slight pang of disappointment to vibrate through her. "Of course. You must be Griff's cousin Lara."

He said it the right way, she noticed, with two *ah* sounds.

"It's short for Larissa," she admitted, rolling her eyes. "Instead of 007 or Dirty Harry, I think my mother had a thing for Dr. Zhivago."

For the first time in her life she knew what it was like to see an actual twinkle come to someone's eyes. "Well, and a good thing, too," he said, wiggling his eyebrows suggestively. "Those Bond girls, at least, went by some pretty racy names."

Now Lara laughed, which brought a look of such pleasure to his face that she dropped her gaze and fumbled with the stethoscope case. It occurred to her that she was no longer the least apprehensive, even though her voice was definitely breathless as she asked, "You know Griff?"

"Sure do. I'm proud to call him one of my best friends." He sat back on his heels. "That was why, when Griff mentioned he had a cousin in Dallas who'd gotten licensed as a physician's assistant and was looking for a job, I started bugging him to get you down here for the Bridgewater Clinic."

"*You're* Griff's boss?" His stock with her went up another ten points. Her cousin had told her it had been the idea of the rancher he worked for to fill the vacancy with a P.A. when Dr. Becker retired, instead of with a full-time doctor. To treat serious cases, a physician would drive out from Houston on a part-time basis. The arrangement would save everyone time and money. Most of all, though, it would provide less-well-off members of the community with better health care, since Griff's boss had also volunteered to pay her salary.

"Well, I don't think of myself as his boss," he said, still sitting on his haunches in front of her. "As my ranch foreman, Griff's more like my partner, is how I see it. And my name—since I'm thinkin' you're still wondering—is actually Connor."

He extended his hand, and Lara had no choice but to take it. Yes, she thought, his touch was definitely warm, reaching clear up her arm and kindling something in her chest.

"I have to say it, Lara," Connor added candidly, his gaze sure and sincere, "I'm sure glad you've arrived. We need you here in Bridgewater."

It was hopeless. No matter how much she'd tried not to, Lara finally blushed. Hard. She didn't have to see her face lit up as bright as a Christmas bulb to know it was, because that's what she invariably did when an attractive male showed her the least bit of attention. Which usually then led to her running like a jackrabbit in the other direction.

Yet with Connor, she felt the exact opposite. As if for once she actually was right where she needed to be.

How strange that it should be this way, though. She'd had so many doubts about how she would like leaving Dallas to run the tiny medical clinic in this town that the mere thought always caused a certain ache deep in her heart.

But her cousin had told her that things had changed in the twenty-some years since she and her mother had left to make a new life away from the painful memories. The man who'd caused them both so much grief no longer wielded the kind of power over Bridgewater and the entire county as he had back then. There was a whole different feeling around town, Griff said—as if it was all, to turn a phrase, water under the bridge.

And with as sincere a reception as this one, from the man who was responsible for bringing her here as a way of helping the less fortunate citizens in the area to live better lives… Well, maybe Griff was right, Lara mentally admitted, and things *had* changed—things that had not so much to do with Bridgewater, Texas, as they had to do with one Lara Dearborn and how she felt immediately at ease with this man in one of the most unique moments of her life.

And if so, she was glad. Glad she'd taken the chance to come back. Because here she could make a difference, be involved in the rewarding work of running this small medical clinic in between the doctor's visits each week, taking care of whatever cases came through the door—illnesses and injuries, checkups and immunizations. Seeing to people's needs. Being needed.

Yes, she was glad the past was past and, as she stared into Connor's deep brown eyes, glad that the future was the future, with all its possibilities.

She smiled, feeling her face grow even redder. She didn't care, because Connor's dimples deepened, making her wonder what it would be like to curl up in one of those hollows. Like sheer heaven, she ventured to guess.

"I bet you've come to take a look around where you'll be spending most of your waking hours," he said.

"That's exactly why I'm here," she answered matter-of-factly, as if his knowing her purpose didn't surprise her in the least.

"Then may I have the honor of taking you on the dollar tour?" He stood, and something about how he held out his hand to her made it seem as if they were partners, completely attuned to each other.

Without hesitation, Lara slid her fingers into that warm, firm grip of his.

"I'm right beside you," she said.

"I'VE BEEN WAXING the wood floors, trying to spruce the place up a bit before you got here," Connor explained, opening the door to one of the examining rooms and flicking on the light as Lara craned her neck over his shoulder to get a view into what she'd already come to think of as *her* clinic.

She followed him through the doorway, and he stood to one side as excitement bubbled through her with the effervescence of a babbling brook. Her gaze made a thorough journey around the room. Contrary to his claim, on first glance the place looked to be spick-and-span, so any cleaning Connor was doing had to be purely cosmetic, she guessed.

The October sun streamed in through the blinds, bathing everything in a warm, inviting light. The leather examining table had a fresh swatch of white tissue running down its middle, ready for the next patient. A blood pressure cuff was mounted next to the table, with an eye chart on the wall directly opposite it. On the other side, a variety of instruments and supplies were lined up on the bright white Formica counter: an otoscope; tongue depressors and cotton balls in clear apothecary jars; even a digital thermometer, she was happy to note. Completing the picture was the neatly stacked display of literature on nutrition, prenatal care and childhood diseases.

"It's not the most up-to-date facility," Connor said apologetically from behind her. She pivoted to find him leaning back against the examining table a few feet away. And, it seemed to her, watching more than her reaction with interest. His gaze dropped momentarily to her smiling mouth before leisurely traveling back up to her eyes in a manner that had Lara swinging away from him again with a nervous flutter, feeling a little less comfortable than she had with him moments before.

"That doesn't bother me," she assured him.

"Maybe not, but that's another reason why, since old Doc Becker retired a year and a half ago, the town hasn't been able to get a physician who wants to practice out here full-time," Connor observed. "Doc's nurse, Bev Jefferson, has been doin' what she can in between, making sure anyone that needs to gets in to see the new doctor when he's here on Tuesdays and Fridays. But we've felt the lack of someone living here, being a part of the community. The lack of someone people know and trust."

She gave the hot and cold water knobs on the small stainless-steel sink a testing twist. Connor must have noticed, as she did, that the faucet was dripping, for he came up behind her and, reaching around her—and brushing his arm against her shoulder in the process— tried the fixtures himself.

"H-have many people been going without medical care?" Lara asked as she sidestepped away from his touch. His closeness, she was beginning to realize, made her feel giddy and out of control. It wouldn't have been that much of a stretch for her to turn into his embrace and seek a kiss.

"What needs to get done is getting done, I suppose." Connor answered her question readily enough as he leaned back against the cabinet, his hands propped on either side of him on the counter edge. Thankfully, he seemed not to have noticed her nervousness. "But it's my understanding that what the doctor did best was seein' to whatever troubles, health or otherwise, people brought him. I didn't experience it firsthand, since I only moved to the area about when Doc retired."

Lara cast a surprised look at him. "You mean you're not a native?" she asked.

"No. Oh, I was born in Bridgewater, but I spent most of my life in Fort Worth with my mother." His mouth tightened briefly, decreasing the depth of his dimples, but not by much. Then he revealed with quiet dignity, "My folks split up when I was four."

Just like that, her heart went out to him, causing Lara to forget her discomfiture. And causing her to do something uncharacteristic. She reached out and laid her palm on the back of Connor's hand as it gripped the edge of the counter. "I... It wasn't my intent to bring up a painful subject, Connor."

"It's not painful, not anymore," he replied, his brown eyes warming again. Turning toward her, he pressed his other hand over hers. "It's just...there, you know?"

She *did* know. It was on the tip of her tongue to reveal a little of her own story, which was not so very different from his. Her usual reserve, though, held her back.

Still, she realized, another link of immediate understanding had somehow been forged between her and Connor. She honestly had no idea how much of her background Griff had told him, if anything. Whatever the case, it was apparent to Lara that Connor had come to terms with the events of his life, as she believed herself to have done. Understood, too, that they had to, if they were to be free to lead happy lives.

"I can see why Griff likes working for you," she said candidly.

Now it was Connor's turn to redden with pleasure. "I'm glad to hear he does. He's only worked for me for less than a year, but he's gotten to be indispensable. Truth be told, ranching's new to me."

His revelation struck Lara as another fact a little on the sensitive side, and that Connor would feel comfortable divulging another personal detail about himself thrilled her to her toes. If she'd known it was this easy to get to know a man, she might have tried it long ago.

Yet she knew this was no ordinary situation, and that this was no ordinary man.

"Well, even if you are new to ranching, I can't believe you aren't good at it," she said, again with candidness. She didn't remove her hand from his grasp, even when his fingers tightened and tugged her an inch or two closer.

"Believe me, I've got a lot to learn," he said in a voice that had dropped half a dozen decibels, making the atmosphere in the room seem abruptly intimate. "But somehow I suddenly don't mind any job I've got on my plate, now that you've come to town."

"Me?" Lara's throat had gone sandpaper dry in an instant, as her gaze homed in of its own volition on his wide mouth. Was she crazy or was he about to kiss her? "What have I got to do with anything?"

"I don't know, Lara," he said softly, shifting an inch closer to her. She swallowed, her gaze lifting once again to his, and saw it in his eyes. No, she wasn't crazy. But yes, she might be about to kiss a man she'd only just met. "You're just...*you.*"

"M-me?" she repeated—crazily. Because he *was* going to kiss her—his mouth was a breath from hers—and she had a feeling she wasn't going to mind a bit.

Soft his kiss was, though hardly tentative. Exploring, wondering, was more like it. Lara didn't close her eyes, and neither did Connor, she noticed, as her own wonder expanded and warmed her, like the sun coming out from behind a dark, dense cloud that had hung over her for a long, long time.

His hand lifted to cup her jaw and draw her even closer. But first she needed to know....

"What is it, Connor?" she whispered. "About me, I mean?"

He smiled against her lips. "It's just that… somehow I feel I can pretty much be myself with you, without Tanglewood and all that comes with it hanging over my head."

Even under the spell of Connor's kiss Lara heard the faint alarm bell sound in the back of her mind. She drew back infinitesimally. "Tanglewood?"

"It's my family's ranch."

"You mean the one…out on the Brazos River? The one that covers half the county?"

Even though she'd not blinked an eye, wariness suddenly infused Connor's whole being. "Yes."

Now she did draw away, almost automatically, and even though her thoughts were whirling, she could see what even that small retreat did to this man, could see the pain darkening his liquid eyes. Yet there was that wariness, too, that told her he knew something wasn't right.

"Then that must mean that your…that your last name is…"

Connor glanced away briefly, his jaw tightening visibly, as if he'd just endured a shooting pain through his vitals. Still, he answered readily enough. "It's Brody."

She couldn't keep the shock—no, the downright horror—out of her voice as she whispered, "Then…that makes you Mick Brody's son, right?"

He hesitated, then nodded. "Yes."

Lara stepped away from him as if stung. Oh, she knew she had no right to feel betrayed, but she did. By Grill, to be sure, who *knew* her story and how difficult it had been all these years, more for her mother than herself. But Lara also felt betrayed by fate, for putting her into this position at the precise moment she'd let down her guard with a man.

Real fear hit her then with the impact of a Mack truck. Did Connor know who she was and what had happened? How could he, though, and be able to stand here before her without expecting her to feel *some* kind of outrage toward him?

Because the past *wasn't* water under the bridge! How could it be when it was Mick Brody who'd been the one to destroy her father and drive him away from her and her mother, leaving the two of them to carry on alone?

Chapter Two

Try as he might, Connor couldn't banish the sense of futility that engulfed him as Lara Dearborn stared at him in shock, as if a ghost had risen up behind him.

Actually, wasn't his father's reputation exactly that—a specter that shadowed him wherever he went, whatever he did? For once again he was accused and judged before he even had a chance to prove his case: he was *not* like Mick Brody!

Even blindfolded Justice, though, couldn't have missed the look that was firmly lodged in Lara's eyes. How many times had he himself seen the verdict on the faces of nearly every person in Bridgewater at one moment or another? They doubted his every motive, were wary of his every move, as if they suspected he'd rob them blind if they weren't ever vigilant.

But that wasn't the worst. It was when he

saw a certain fear lurking in the back of people's gazes that he died inside. Fear that if they *did* trust him a little, he was still, underneath it all, too much of a Brody to keep from giving in to his nature sometime down the road, and playing them for fools. Or worse.

Yet he *had* made progress with the townspeople in the past six months. The effort had been grueling and about as discouraging as a situation could get—he'd been close to giving up dozens of times. But little by little he was gaining people's trust, and the watchfulness was retreating from their gazes. It wasn't his imagination. In fact, it struck him only now how much he'd come to expect having to prove himself to people before being trusted. For when he'd experienced the opposite right now with Lara, he'd unconsciously found it as freeing as shaking off shackles he'd been weighed down with since time began.

And that was why now, seeing all those emotions—and more—flood Lara's soft gray eyes, it was worse than ever.

For as it turned out, she was just like everyone else.

"Yes," he said more strongly, mustering the commitment to uncompromised honesty that had gotten him through so far. "I'm Mick Brody's son. I see his reputation precedes me," he added, unable to keep a wry twist out of his voice. "All the way to Dallas."

He wondered who'd told Lara about his father. Griff? Somehow Connor couldn't believe it. His foreman had been his staunchest supporter since coming to work at Tanglewood six months ago, right after Connor had taken over management of the ranch. Right after his father had been arrested, tried and sent to prison a convicted murderer. Leaving Connor to face a whole county of people who had come to put the name of Brody in the same category as they would a rattlesnake.

"I...I was born here, too," Lara said in a muted voice. "My mother and I had to leave when I was four years old, too."

He'd have found the charity within him to feel some sympathy for her, but he was too steamed that she obviously was holding on to an opinion about his father that she'd formed when she was barely out of diapers. "Then you don't know the latest. Or do you?"

"No," she admitted softly.

"Last year it was discovered that my dad was responsible for the death of the ranch manager on the Bar G almost a decade ago. Seems the foreman had stolen away my dad's sweetheart some years before."

Connor took a breath, then went on without

a trace of sugarcoating. "It's only because we could afford the best damn defense attorney in Texas that Dad got off with a thirty-year sentence, with the possibility of parole after serving ten. Otherwise there's a good bet he'd be sitting on death row at Huntsville right now or, at the very least, spending the rest of his life in prison."

Lara's pink mouth formed an aghast O, which only succeeded in making Connor's spirits plunge to an even greater depth. Because it struck him that just moments ago—only a few ticks of the clock—he'd felt so at ease with this woman he'd dared be so bold as to kiss her.

He at least wanted to touch her again, though he had no illusions she'd react as she had before, with that gloriously rosy infusion of color over her creamy cheeks that was like the dawn breaking. Her short blond hair, styled in the tousled way that was popular these days, as if she'd just gotten out of bed, begged for fingers to be run through the silken strands. In fact, the golden wisps framing her face in a halo, combined with those bedroom eyes and full, pouting lips, made her look as if indeed she'd only moments before been roused from a deep sleep—with exactly the soul-stirring kiss he'd been a split second away from giving her.

Something of what he was thinking must have shown in his eyes, for fear again appeared in the back of hers. Although, he couldn't help noticing, it was more complex than the apprehension he'd seen there before. Less to do with who he was as a Brody than with what he was—a man. And either way, he couldn't see it boding well for him.

Still, he couldn't quite forget those few moments of closeness between them. It hadn't been his imagination!

He'd bent his gaze on Lara again, meaning to ask her about that, when a voice came from the front of the clinic. "Hello? Is anyone here?"

Stifling his frustration, Connor pivoted and stepped into the hallway. Down the corridor stood a slightly familiar man, holding a bundled-up child against his shoulder.

"Oh, Mr. Brody. It's me, Russ Dayton—I live out near the plastics plant?"

"Of course. I remember meeting you when the county board of supervisors' task force I was on came out for that inspection." Connor walked forward to take the man's hand. Russ shook his briefly before placing his palm back against the child's nape.

"Are things goin' a bit better for you now that those emission standards are being enforced?" Connor asked.

"Sure are, Mr. Brody. We don't get the problems we had before in the neighborhood with breathing, and our eyes don't sting half the time, either."

"Good." Of course, he'd only been fixing what his father, whose place Connor had taken on the board, had neglected to take care of years ago. In any case, at least he could look *those* people in the eye and not have what he saw there make him feel like Public Enemy Number One. "And call me Connor, all right?"

Russ nodded. "That ain't why I'm here today, though. I need help for my boy here, and I'd heard that new gal you hired was comin' to town soon—"

"I'm Lara Dearborn, the new physician's assistant." Lara spoke up from behind Connor. "Is there something I can help you with?"

Connor glanced down at her as she strode past him. The change in her from a few moments before astounded him so thoroughly it set him back a step.

Was this the same Lara Dearborn? With him, she'd been as skittish as a wild mustang. Now, however, she was all efficiency, exuding an air of competence that was somewhat akin to that of a five-star general, and making Connor all the more certain he'd mistaken the significance of the moment between them.

"I sure hope so, ma'am," Russ said with obvious relief at seeing her. He tugged back the edge of the worn patchwork quilt to reveal a boy of about five, Connor guessed. The little one's red hair was plastered in damp patches to his scalp as he slept fitfully against his father's shoulder, a bright spot of crimson coloring his otherwise pale cheek.

"Bobby's had a bad fever goin' on two days now, and he's complainin' of being sick at his stomach," Russ explained to Lara. "He's got some kind of fierce headache, too, he said. I think he might've caught a bug that was goin' round with his cousins while we were visitin' them a week or so ago. It's probably somethin' that needs to run its course, but I thought since you were here, you might could do somethin' for him?" Worry creased his forehead. "I hate to see him suffer if he don't have to."

"I'm sure I can help in some way," she reassured the man without a second of hesitation. "Let's get Bobby in here to the examining room, where I can have a look at him."

The two of them seemed to have forgotten all about Connor, who watched Russ follow Lara to the room they'd just come from. "Have you brought him in to the clinic for treatment before, Mr. Dayton?" she asked over her shoulder.

"Yeah—he's always gotten his vaccinations here, and before she passed on, his mother used bring him in 'bout every month, it seemed, for some kind of illness or another. You know how little kids are forever comin' down with stuff, Dr. Dearborn."

Connor trailed after the two of them, but stopped short of entering the examination room, instead standing awkwardly in the doorway to observe the action going on within.

Lara had pulled two latex gloves from a blue-and-white box on the counter and was tugging them on. "I'm not a physician, Mr. Dayton. And you can call me Lara."

"Well, it don't seem proper, but all right... Lara."

She smiled up at Russ Dayton. Actually, she submerged him in the caring glow of her smile in a way that caused a rash of jealousy in Connor, for she'd looked the same way at him a moment ago.

Yet he was greatly afraid that that perfect moment—when the trust had been extended on both sides and acceptance given—was forever lost to both Lara and him. If it had ever been real in the first place.

Perhaps it hadn't. Real trust didn't spring fully formed from anyone's heart—except, perhaps, the trust a child had for a parent. And Connor knew, with abundant clarity, just how tenuous that connection could be, too.

"Is there anything I can do to help?" he blurted out, feeling about as superfluous as a sixth toe. But he had to ask. He had to try.

At his question, Lara frowned, and he could see her come out of her professional mode and return to the wary woman he'd met a few minutes ago. The doubt he noted in her soft gray gaze about killed him.

"I know you barely know me from Adam and believe I'm as bad as Cain," he added pointedly, "but I could probably find my way around the clinic here and get you whatever you needed—like little Bobby's records. Or if you needed it, Bev's number so a trained person could come in and help you." Connor spread his hands. "I mean, I do have my uses, however small."

She surprised him by actually smiling. "As a matter of fact…if you *could* find a file on Bobby that has his medical history, I'd appreciate it." She chewed on her lower lip in a way that had Connor's thoughts turning once again to that imagined kiss. "And there's no need to call in the nurse on her day off. But without her, I may need you to give me a hand locating things." Her gaze met his inquiringly. "If you don't mind helping, that is."

"Not a bit," Connor answered quickly. He hadn't a clue where to find anything, but he'd give the effort his best shot.

Because as far as he knew, they still couldn't convict a man for trying, could they?

BY THE TIME he'd located Bobby Dayton's file and returned to the examining room, Lara was well into doing a physical on the child, who was at least awake now, though clearly groggy from his fever. His skin shone damply, and he was shivering even within the warmth of his father's arms as Lara moved a stethoscope over his chest, having unbuttoned his shirt.

Connor set the manila folder on the counter. "I've got his records right here."

The file hadn't been easy to locate. Bev definitely had a system, but it seemed to Connor she'd invented it on one of her more whimsical days. Once he got the chance, he'd check out software packages for medical office management, then set one up and train Bev on how to get all the patients' information into a database and maintain it. The office would run much more efficiently that way, not to mention be safer for patients should another situation like today's come along.

It was at least one thing he was capable of and could do to help.

Speaking of capable, even in jeans, tennis shoes and an old Texas Rangers jersey, Lara fit the bill of efficiency to a T. He was still having a hard time getting the two impressions he had of her to jibe in his mind.

"Ow! That hurts!" Bobby cried, bringing Connor back to the present. Lara had set the boy back on the examining table, and his complaint had come as a result of her gently prodding his abdomen.

"I'm sorry, Bobby," she murmured. "You've got some pain in your tummy, then, do you?"

The boy nodded up at her, obviously wide-awake now and looking as worried as his father, who stood at his shoulder, soothing back the boy's damp hair with his palm.

Lara left off her examination to sit on the doctor's stool and page through the boy's file, her stethoscope around her neck. "You said the symptoms began two days ago?"

"Yes, ma'am," Russ replied.

"And how long ago were you visiting your... was it your cousins?"

"It's my wife's sister's family in Oklahoma. We've gone up there every September to camp out in the Arbuckle Mountains near Davis since Bobby was just a young 'un."

Although little changed about Lara, Connor could tell she'd gone instantly on alert at Russ's revelation. With great deliberateness, she closed the file and set it back on the counter.

"And how long ago was that?" she asked again, her soft voice perfectly calm.

"Oh, a week, week and a half ago."

"Was Bobby out playing in any wooded areas that you know of, Russ?" Still sitting, she wheeled the stool back over to the boy's side. "Or was there a dog around?"

The other man shrugged, apparently missing the change in Lara that Connor had noted—and he was quickly getting a clue as to what she suspected. "Shoot, yeah, all the kids were out hikin' and fishin' till they were fall-down tired. At least until one of my nephews come down with a flu bug, like I said. We had to cut the trip short to get him home."

As Russ was talking, Connor noticed that Lara had gently pulled off Bobby's cowboy boots and socks and rolled up the cuffs of his jeans. She bent over the boy, running her hands over his skin as she scrutinized his ankles. Then she unbuttoned the cuffs of his long-sleeved shirt and did the same to his wrists and forearms.

"Of course, that flu was one of those twenty-four-hour kinds that takes the stuffin' out of you while it's in your system but don't hang around that long, like this one seems to be doin' with Bobby—"

"There it is!" Lara suddenly exclaimed. She indicated to Russ a place above her thumbnail. Stepping closer to peer at where she pointed, Connor saw a bunch of pale pink spots, like a rash, on the inside of the boy's left wrist. She pressed the pad of her thumb over them for a count of five before releasing the pressure. The spots briefly disappeared, then came back slowly.

Lara sat back. "It looks as if Bobby may have contracted not a flu bug but another kind of bug while in Oklahoma—a tick that's given him Rocky Mountain spotted fever."

The man paled, and Connor spontaneously set a comforting hand on his shoulder, which seemed to allay Russ's fears not the least. The disease wasn't that common in Texas, but everyone knew Oklahoma had one of the highest incidences of it in the United States. And the reason people feared it was because death was not an uncommon result of the disease. It was pretty difficult to diagnose—and often, even if it was caught, irreparable damage was done to the victim.

"Is he…will he be all right, Lara?" Russ whispered, ignoring Connor completely as he clutched his son against him, his gaze fixed on the woman across the examining table from him. "He's not going to…going to—" He swallowed painfully, unable to say the word. "I swear, I thought it was just a flu bug! You've got to believe me!"

"Daddy?" Bobby said uncertainly, fear tightening his small mouth as he looked from his father to Lara and back again. "What's goin' on, Daddy?"

"I assure you," she said, "there's no reason to panic—"

"Just tell me if my boy's gonna be all right!" Russ begged, shaking off Connor's hand. "I—I can't lose him, too!"

She looked up at the man, and her clear-eyed gaze was like a silver lining in storm clouds, calming everything and everyone.

"Yes, Mr. Dayton. Bobby will be just fine. We've caught the disease in time. I'll draw some blood to make sure, and it'll be up to a physician to confirm the diagnosis, but we'll put Bobby on antibiotics right away."

She smoothed the boy's hair back from his forehead in a gesture that had the effect of comforting both father and child. "You're not to worry," she told them both.

It blew Connor away. It wasn't that he hadn't thought she would be thoroughly competent. But she was obviously able to impart something more important than competence: she was able to convey calmness and optimism, which would inspire trust in the townspeople—the kind of trust they would need to have in their health-care giver. A trust he would never be able to inspire, he realized, no matter how long he tried.

It made him realize what had been needling him since Russ Dayton and his son had walked in the door, interrupting him and Lara in a moment Connor now knew would never be recovered. If this woman, whose integrity shone from her, judged him as Mick Brody's son, knowing little else about him, and found him guilty, what real chance did he have of truly making the local townspeople trust him?

The futility of it was crushing.

"How can I thank you, Lara?" Russ said, abruptly grasping her gloved hand in his. The unsolicited contact caught her off guard, Connor noted, although she continued to smile.

"No thanks is needed, Mr. Dayton. Honest."

Then Russ Dayton turned to him, of all people. "And thank you, Connor."

"Me?" he exclaimed. "Why thank me?"

Tears had sprung to the father's eyes. "Seein' as how we din't have no doctor in town and I couldn't've got off work too easy durin' the week to take Bobby to see one, I would've waited even longer than I already did to see if he'd get better on his own. And if you hadn't hired Lara here to take Doc Becker's place, I *would* have waited, who knows how much longer!"

A moment of silence ensued as the specter of tragedy hovered close. It wasn't the first time Connor had experienced such a feeling—although in the past it had always been as a lingering effect of his father's actions. This time, however, the shadow passed by as if repelled by an opposing force.

Connor shook his head. "There's no need to thank me, Russ, really," he said brusquely, denying his right to any compliment. "Anyone in my place with my resources would have done the same."

"No, anyone wouldn't've, Connor—meanin' your dad." Russ gave a firm nod as he gathered up his precious cargo—his son—in his arms again. "I don't think I'm tellin' tales out of school saying that a lot of people in Bridgewater think you're only doin' what you're doin' 'cause you're trying to make up for some of the grief he's caused over the years. I guess my opinion is it don't matter why. You're bringin' about change here—*good* change. And that's never a thing to reject for any reason."

Hearing Russ's dead-on assessment of the situation he'd been dealing with for months—and the suspicions he'd held of what people thought of him—might have goaded Connor deeply at one time. But now he simply wondered how Russ's pronouncement made him appear to Lara. As little as she knew of him, did *she* think him the kind of man whose deeds were self-serving, meant either to try to make up for the harm his father had done or to make himself feel better about it, rather than being motivated from a sincere desire to help people?

Looking at her as she sat before him, studying him pensively, he couldn't tell. And he wasn't sure if he wanted to know.

Because he had a feeling Lara would know the difference—and unlike Russ Dayton, *would* care.

Chapter Three

"Hades's ladies, Griff, why didn't you tell me who your boss was?" Lara demanded.

She braced her palms against the doorjamb as she blocked her cousin from entering the small bungalow she'd rented for her home.

Griff Corbin merely gave her that signature unruffled look of his from beneath the battered brim of his black Stetson.

"Hello to you, too, cuz," he drawled. He shoved at the basket he'd had tucked under one arm, and she was forced to abandon her stance to take it. "Mom's sent some cleanin' products she thought you might need, plus a casserole and a couple jars of green beans she canned a few weeks ago, since she doubted you'd be able to do much for cookin' till you got unpacked. She'd've brought it by herself but she's goin' hell for bear tryin' to get her quilt done for the fall church bazaar, and you can imagine any failure on that score would rank right up there with sitting back and lettin' the ozone layer go to pot. No way would she have a quilt of hers up for raffle that didn't have every stitch in place."

All this was delivered calmly as Griff unceremoniously placed his hands under Lara's arms and lifted her out of his path. Then he strolled past her into her own house, with that hitched gait of his. It was the only outward reminder of the injury he'd suffered as a boy, when he'd been gored by a bull.

But she knew he bore inner scars. They both did, for different reasons. And much as she'd like to believe those old wounds were truly healed, this afternoon had surely proved her wrong, hadn't it?

The thought tempered her next words as she followed him down the hallway and into the kitchen. "If you're thinking to share your mom's home cooking and canned green beans with me, both come with a price. I need help moving the dresser in my bedroom to the opposite wall and putting the bed there instead. And I don't like where the sofa is in the living room, even if I haven't figured out the best place for it yet."

She glanced around, trying to find a spot to set her aunt's care package among the clutter. It was a difficult task. The movers had come only yesterday, and there were boxes stacked in every room, along with a haphazard arrangement of furniture. Trying to go from one end of the house to the other was like negotiating a maze.

Not that she had that many belongings. She'd lived with her mother in their apartment through college at Southwestern Medical Center in Dallas, and it had been by financial necessity a small place. People always seemed to discover, though, just how much stuff they'd accumulated only when they moved.

She finally gave up and set her aunt's basket on top of a stack of boxes. Rooting around, she located two plates—although they were only saucer-size—and forks. She dished up her aunt's corned beef hash and canned beans, giving both plates of food a zap in the microwave—which she had to relocate in order to plug into an outlet.

Meanwhile Griff pulled a Lone Star beer for himself out of the cooler in the corner and fetched a Coke for her.

"Thank you for arranging for this house for me, by the way," Lara told her cousin.

"Don't thank me so much as Mom," Griff replied as he moved her blender to one side and settled himself in the space he'd cleared on her counter. "She's the one who wangled old Tessie Calloway down from five hundred a month to three-fifty."

"It would have been a bargain at any price." She gave a glance around. "I've always wanted a house instead of an apartment. It was one of the dreams Mom and I had for years and years."

At the thought of her mother and some of the other dreams they'd shared, that familiar tightening squeezed at Lara's heart. "I can't wait for her to see it," she added.

"That would be the point, I think. My mom's hopin' if she gets you back to Bridgewater that maybe Pauline will follow." He peered at her from under the brim of his Stetson. "It'd sure be nice for both of them to have the other close."

Griff's mother, Frannie, and Lara's mother were sisters-in-law, and ever since Griff's father, Pauline's brother, had died a few years ago, the two women had achieved a certain closeness. It was born, Lara was sure, of having lost the love of one's life too soon, although in entirely different ways.

And for very different reasons.

"I hate to break it to you, Griff, but getting Mom back here permanently? That's not going to happen," Lara said gently. "She was all for me coming down here to take charge of the clinic. But she's not coming back."

She looked her cousin squarely in the eye. "And you know why. You didn't answer my question, Griff. Why didn't you tell me who your boss was?"

"Why would I?" he asked with what struck her as supreme obtuseness.

She rose and set her barely touched plate in the sink with a clatter. "Because he's Mick Brody's son, that's why! Not only that, he's the one who got you to talk me into coming down here! Griff, does he *know* what his father did to my family?"

"No—and no one's gonna bring it up, either," Griff said sternly. "It's ancient history, Lara, dead and buried. Connor is nothin' like his dad."

He gestured with his fork, poking the air in front of him. "Fact is, he was the one who found out and brought to the sheriff's attention that his daddy was responsible for nearly causing a terrible accident on the Bar G. And it couldn't've been easy for him to stand there and see it revealed that his own kin had killed an innocent man those years ago. Why, Deke Larrabie himself, whose daddy Mick killed, doesn't hold that against Connor, so I'm thinkin' you'd be one hard case to do it."

Griff jammed a forkful of beans into his mouth and chewed furiously. "Besides, Mick Brody is payin' for his sins right now in prison."

"Not all of them, Griff," Lara said quietly but firmly. "Not all of them."

She stared out the window to the small, tidy backyard that she'd hoped to make her imprint on. Though it was late October, here in southern Texas there would be plenty of time to plant daffodil bulbs along the fence line for a spring bloom, lots of opportunities to enjoy evenings outside under the shade of the still-flowering mimosa tree.

Yet for a brief instant, she wished she hadn't come back to Bridgewater. It would have been infinitely easier to have stayed in Dallas and taken a position in one of the physician's offices there. She'd had several offers, at a much higher rate of pay than this one. But she had been drawn by the chance to do exactly the kind of work she'd done today.

It had been a gift, she realized, having Russ Dayton bring his son in at that exact moment. Because it *had* been at the top of her mind to run, to leave right then and there, rather than deal with the confusing feelings Connor Brody produced in her.

On one side, there was her aversion to his

mere presence in her life, as if somehow any slim connection to the Brodys had the potential to harm her and her family. She didn't think her mistrust of his motives was entirely a product of the history between the two families, either. Russ had certainly seemed to strike a sore spot with his observation about how the townspeople viewed Connor's actions; his handsome, expressive face had become stiff with irritation.

But then there'd been that closeness that had sprung up between Connor and her with such swiftness and ease. That and the recognition of how important her mission here was. How important *their* mission was, for he was responsible for recognizing the need in the community. And as Russ Dayton had pointed out, what difference did it make why Connor did what he did, if he brought about real and positive change?

Yet Lara knew the answer to that question: it made a difference to *her,* very much so, although she couldn't have said why.

A bell chimed at that moment, making her turn in confusion toward the microwave before realizing it was the sound of her doorbell. Who could be at the door? Hopefully it wasn't a neighbor with a cheery welcome and a desire to chat, Lara thought as she walked back to the front of the house, dodging boxes and a stray ottoman. She just wasn't up to dealing with more strangers right now.

She got her wish. It wasn't a friendly faced neighbor at her front door.

It was Connor Brody. *Hades's ladies.*

The late-afternoon sun set his profile into relief and limned his strongest features: his jawline, his straight nose, which she only just now noticed, and of course those dimples, which were never completely absent from his face even when his smile was.

Such as now, as they bracketed the straight line of his mouth. "Saw Griff's pickup in the driveway," he said with a grim nod in that direction. "I'd borrowed his toolbox this afternoon to do that work over at the clinic. I'm not a natural with a wrench, but I did manage to fix the leaky faucet. It'll take someone with some serious planing tools, though, to fix that sticky front door for you."

"Th-thank you," Lara said helplessly. He looked so serious. So subdued. And so thoroughly different from the open, smiling man who'd first greeted her at the clinic this afternoon.

Yes, she missed his smile—already.

"Hey there, Connor." Griff came up behind her. "Headin' back to Tanglewood?"

Connor nodded tersely. "I was just tellin' Lara I put your tools in the back of your truck. Didn't know if you'd need 'em before you came to work on Monday. You know, what with Lara movin' in."

"No doubt she's got a list of things as long as my arm worked up for me to do," Griff said with fond tolerance, even ruffling her hair as if she were a six-year-old. She shot him a dirty look, which he met with a thoroughly perverse one of his own. "Say, didn't you mention needin' a bunch of furniture moved this evening?" he asked.

She caught on to his motive right away. "Just a dresser and a sofa. A-and my bed." She didn't dare glance at Connor or she'd redden in embarrassment. "But you and I can manage those ourselves just fine."

"Don't be so sure," Griff countered easily. "From what you said, you're wafflin' around about where you want stuff to go." He drew his palm across his chin, causing a rasp from his five-o'clock shadow. "It'd go a whole lot quicker with an extra man. How about it, Connor?"

Lara ventured a peek at Connor under cover of brushing a dead leaf off her front step with the toe of her shoe. His face was bemused.

"Maybe I better just move on down the road," he said.

"To what?" her cousin protested. Lara guessed Griff had about sixty pounds on her and at least six inches in height, but she was up to wrestling him to the ground, she was so furious with him. "Elda's got the night off from Tanglewood, so it'd be your usual Saturday night special of runny scrambled eggs and half-frozen hash browns. There's plenty of my mom's homemade corned beef hash in the kitchen, which I understand is the reward for helpin' out—*isn't* it, Lara?"

"Yes," she answered between gritted teeth.

Connor must have noticed her discomfiture. "Of course I'd like to be of help to your kin any way I could, Griff, after all you've done for me," he said. "But it's pretty clear to me that Lara's not comfortable with me. And especially with my comin' into her house. A person ought to feel their home is a safe haven."

Lara stared at Connor outright. She had to give him credit; he didn't shy away from people or the truth about his father. And he did so with such a fine dignity that she couldn't help but be stirred by the burden that rested upon his shoulders through no fault of his own.

With a parting nod, he turned to go.

"Actually, Connor," she said before she could think about it, "I—I'd appreciate any help you could lend us."

He swung back around, his face clearing with such swiftness it tugged at her heart— in a way that both drew her to him and made her want to flee as far as she could from him and the feelings he stirred up.

"If you're sure...?" he said.

Oh, she was anything but sure! "Of course."

"Then it'd be my pleasure," he answered, and Lara stepped aside as the son of her sworn enemy entered her home.

YES, HAVING CONNOR in her home was disconcerting, to say the least. Yet Lara knew having him in her bedroom, where the three of them stood now, having polished off Aunt Frannie's hash, was downright unnerving.

First of all, she hadn't made her bed that morning, and somehow having Connor see the bedclothes, rumpled and tossed as if she'd just risen from a night's sleep, seemed so intimate it made her blush to the roots of her blond hair.

Not only that, but south Texas was experiencing what seemed to be a spell of Indian summer; even though the sun had set, the temperature remained in the eighties. Unfortunately, her landlord had already put the window air-conditioning unit away in the garage, leaving the house muggy and close.

To top it off, Lara had left the moving to be done in the bedroom till last, the upshot being that by the time they got to it, both Connor and Griff had worked up a sweat, necessitating the removal of their shirts.

"Here, the bed'll be lighter if I take stuff off of it," she said nervously, practically diving onto the mattress to gather sheets, pillows and covers up in a ball, which she deposited on a wicker armchair in the corner. That was what she needed, she decided—more wicker furniture or something like it. Female furniture that she could blame well move by herself, thank you very much, and none of this having to depend upon a man to do things for her.

Her gesture, she discovered, was for naught. The room seemed to become even smaller as, muscles bulging, Connor lifted one end of the bed, Griff the other, to set it against the opposite wall per her instructions.

Connor stood back, hands at his waist, waiting for her approval of the placement. The problem was, she couldn't have produced a coherent word if she'd wanted to as, in fascination, she watched a trickle of perspiration trail down his strongly defined throat and into the sprinkling of dark hair on his chest.

She tore her gaze away and made herself concentrate on the task at hand.

"No," she finally said. The word came out in a croak. "I'm afraid the bed's not going to work there. I'd like to have it between the windows so the morning sun doesn't come pouring into the room right into my eyes, but the space isn't large enough by half." She bit her lower lip. "And its position there completely interrupts the room's flow."

Both men simply stared at her.

"Oh, stop it," she said. "I've heard you argue for hours on end on the ultrafine points of whether a nylon or hemp catch rope is best for range work, cuz."

"She's got you there, doesn't she, Griff?" Connor said with a laugh that made Lara's stomach do a funny flip. Partly because he had such an attractive laugh and partly because she'd secretly feared she might not ever hear it again.

He indicated the south wall opposite the doorway and perpendicular to the one with windows facing the front of the house. "What about putting the bed here?" he asked. "The sun'll still hit it, but only along the right side—so I guess that solution depends on which side of the bed you like to sleep on."

Lara simply could not help it; her face heated up like a thermometer about to burst. She didn't trust herself to meet Connor's eyes, but couldn't avoid Griff's. His eyebrows shot up with such vigor they nearly dislodged his hat.

"Well, while y'all are deciding where the bed *doesn't* plug the whole room all the hell up, I'll be getting myself another beer," he announced. "You want one, Connor?"

"I'm good for a while yet."

With that, her cousin sauntered out the door. And there she was, standing in her bedroom with a half-naked man who'd just speculated upon the nature of her sleeping habits.

It certainly was a day for firsts, wasn't it?

Yet she could tell that he was in earnest. There was nothing untoward in his manner, not at all. No, anything suggestive in his words had all come from her.

Which meant she had no call to be disappointed.

"What's this?" Connor asked, picking up the simple wooden frame propped against the wall and peering at the items under the glass. "It looks like a set of dog tags and…is that a real Purple Heart?"

Now Lara *really* felt invaded. And more vulnerable than at any other moment in her life. She reached for the frame, taking it from him and pressing it against her chest. Against her heart.

"They're my father's," she said, hoping Connor would ask no more questions.

She wasn't to have her wish. "Did he serve in the military?" he asked, his voice kind.

"Yes," she answered curtly, then some force inside her compelled her to add with a lift of her chin, "in Vietnam. Before I was born."

He stepped closer to her then and, to her surprise, gently tugged the frame from her grasp and bent to examine it again.

Without looking, she knew every detail contained there. The faded color photo of her father in his uniform, the American flag in the background. He'd been four years younger than she was now, just twenty-one, and with the same vulnerability in his eyes that she had often glimpsed in her own in those moments of stark truth when one accidentally catches sight of one's image in a window or mirror and actually sees into the soul reflected there.

Lara wrapped her arms about her middle, watching Connor. At any time, she knew, she could have asked for the frame back and he would have given it to her, would not have pursued looking at her father's things again. Inside her, however, there was a not altogether straightforward need to see his reaction, to have him understand, even a little bit, the kind of man Dooley Dearborn had been.

And what she and her mother had lost when Mick Brody drove him away.

"He served two tours," she said. "Mama told me that he came home from the first and learned that his best friend since childhood had been killed over there three months before."

"They didn't tell him?"

"No." Wordlessly, she held out her hand, and this time he relinquished the frame without hesitation. She simply needed to hold it herself. Or perhaps it was that she needed not to have Connor have more access to that part of her life.

As it was, she could tell he wanted to ask what, then, had compelled her father to return to the war that took his dearest friend from him. Instead Connor simply murmured, "Two tours and a Purple Heart. He must have been a very brave man." She could hear the admiration in his voice. "A great man."

If she were to say anything to Connor about what had happened to her father at the hands of his, Lara knew it must be now. Not to hurt him, but because she could tell that Connor believed her father had died surrounded by his loving family, at peace.

Yet who was to say whether Dooley Dearborn hadn't been dead and gone for many years now? Lara herself had half believed he was ever since she was little. She had learned, however, not to let such feelings show around her mother, for Pauline Dearborn had *not* given up hope that Dooley would return one day.

And that had been the most difficult thing of all for Lara to witness.

It was on the tip of her tongue to make some kind of explanation when Connor glanced up at her, and it was indeed as if she had caught sight not of her own soul, but of his. A certain hunger lurked way back in the recesses of those deep brown eyes, and only then did she remember where his own father was. For she recognized the nature of that hunger almost immediately, was shamed by the self-absorption that had kept her from recognizing it before: to believe in someone that much—as he had never been able to do with Mick Brody.

And that was why, ultimately, Lara decided to say nothing to Connor of what had happened to her father at the hands of Mick Brody. She still didn't trust him at all, but she wasn't quite so certain as before that that couldn't change, although she had no idea how. But Griff had become a convert. So had Russ Dayton.

Lara dropped her chin to stare sightlessly at the photo of her father, which had become as familiar to her as her own face. Whether or not he would succeed in converting the rest of the town, Connor *was* trying to move on as best he could. So should she...at least try to move on, too? She didn't know how she might begin to put what had happened at Mick Brody's hand behind her, but if she continued to hold on to the sins of anyone's father, the single assurance she *could* count on was that she'd never be at peace. Would never be happy.

The thing was, such a fate was perhaps less frightening than trying for forgiveness, only to discover it wasn't within her ken.

Lara blinked rapidly, the image of her father in his dark green uniform blurring suddenly, only to be replaced with one of Connor. For she realized that, without thinking, she'd sought him out as he stood before her. What showed on her face, she didn't know, but whatever he saw seemed to compel him to reach out as he'd done earlier that day and touch her.

It was only a firm grasp of her elbow, but it seemed as intimate—as bonding—as their brief kiss. For in his strong features and stalwart gaze she saw what she'd found there before, in those few moments before she'd discovered who he was. And what demons he himself fought.

Lara wondered, when she said softly, "Yes, he was—a very brave man," whether Connor knew that she was speaking not of Dooley Dearborn, but of him.

She couldn't tell him so, of course. For he was still his father's son. And she was still her father's daughter.

Chapter Four

A stack of patient charts in hand, Lara walked to the front of the clinic, only to find Dolly Parton had invaded her waiting room.

"Hey there, Lara," the country singing star, complete with electric-blue spandex pants and rhinestone-studded platform shoes, greeted her jovially, even as she continued tacking up what looked to be a pin-the-tail-on-the-donkey game on one wall.

"Aunt Frannie?" Lara asked. "Jeez Louise, is that you?"

"Yes, it's me under all this paint and big hair." She grunted as she pushed the tack into the wall. "I figured if this was gonna be a real party for the young 'uns, I'd best get into the act."

"A party—here?" Lara glanced around in puzzlement at the transformation the clinic's foyer was undergoing. A card table had been set up in one corner, where frosted cupcakes with candy corn on top, and a punch bowl, were assembled. A large square of plastic had been laid down on the pine floor, and on top of it was a galvanized steel washbasin with apples floating in the water. Black and orange streamers spiraled from the light fixture to the corners of the ceiling like the spokes of a wheel, and plastic pumpkin-shaped lights blinked merrily around the perimeter of the front plate glass window.

If Lara hadn't already begun to get the picture of what this was all about, the banner taped over the counter confirmed her suspicions. HAPPY HALLOWEEN it proclaimed in yellow-green ectoplasmic lettering.

Aunt Frannie stood back in satisfaction, her own gaze making a tour of the room. "Well. How d'you think it looks?"

"Very nice," Lara told her. "And while I'm thankful for your effort, is there some reason we're having a Halloween party in the clinic this afternoon?"

"Bev didn't tell you?" She gave an impatient huff as she adjusted the cant of her capacious fake bosom, which had begun to list to the left. "I don't know how the woman keeps her balance with these things attached," Frannie marveled with a shake of her bewigged head, obviously referring to the star she impersonated and not Lara's nurse. "I'm like to tump over at any moment."

Lara had to smile. Minus the padding, her aunt was about as spare and without embellishment as the real Dolly was curvaceous and gilded to her eyeballs.

"Obviously Bev told me nothing," Lara said. "Of course, she was under strict orders not to interrupt me while I spent a few hours catching up on patient files." She glanced around for the nurse. "Where *is* Bev, anyway?"

"She took the chance once I got here to run home and get up a costume of her own, plus fetch her electric coffee urn to heat the cider. Connor thought the adults would like somethin' besides punch for refreshment."

Lara's stomach flip-flopped at the mention of that name. "Connor Brody's involved in this?" she asked in even more confusion. "How?"

"It was all his idea, actually. What a nice young man he's turned out to be, despite who his father is."

Aunt Frannie gazed at Lara solemnly, the effect spoiled somewhat by the false eyelash coming loose at the outer corner of one eye. "Griff mentioned you were pretty aggravated with him for not tellin' you Connor was his boss—and yours."

"I didn't have a right to be?" Lara asked mildly.

She slid the files into Bev's In box rather energetically. Since returning to Bridgewater, she still hadn't figured out how she felt about a lot of things, Connor included. She'd certainly developed a grudging respect for the steps he was taking to make up for his father's past sins. But that didn't automatically grant him the kind of trust one reserved for Walter Cronkite.

"We—ell, I wouldn't say that," Frannie replied. "Griff's like his own daddy, often not sayin' anything on a subject for feelin' that things will work themselves out fine if left alone." She shook her head ruefully. "Which sometimes doesn't work to his advantage, I've noticed. But surely you can see Connor Brody's trying his darnedest to make the best of a bad situation—and that's all anyone can expect of another in this world, isn't it?"

Lara crossed her arms. "You're talking about me holding it against Connor that Mick Brody was responsible for driving Dad away, aren't you?" Reaching up, she needlessly straightened the leg of a cardboard skeleton taped to the wall. "I *don't* hold it against him, honestly. But it'd be foolish of me to trust any man without seeing for myself that he's on the up-and-up."

"Actually, I was talkin' about your not holding it against your daddy for leaving," her aunt said gently.

Lara's chin came around sharply. "I don't hold it against Dad for leaving!" she declared. The problem was, her voice sounded a little too adamant even to her own ears. "I mean, he was driven away! If he'd left us on purpose, how could Mom have kept loving him and praying for his return all these years?"

Frannie just looked at her, compassion written on her features. "We all do what we have to do in this life, hon, when it comes to helpin' the people we love deal with their burdens. And sometimes that means lettin' go for a while."

Lara frowned at her aunt. What did Frannie mean, for Pete's sake? That Lara's mother had wanted her father to leave?

Frannie smote her forehead with the heel of her hand, nearly dislodging her platinum-blond wig. "Oh, I just about forgot! I still need to put the scary music on the tape player, and the kids'll be here any second."

She tottered in the four-inch heels she wore

to the back of the clinic just as ten children, all in costume, poured through the door.

Lara welcomed the distraction as, for the next twenty minutes, she dispensed candy from a large bowl on the reception counter to a steady stream of youngsters—the treat, of course, given only after a trick had been performed.

In fact, in all the commotion she forgot about Connor entirely until she raised her head when the front door swung open for the twentieth time, and in he swept.

Lara could only stare, the children's babble fading in her ears. He was dressed in his usual jeans and cowboy boots, but he also had on a black shirt, open at the collar, over which he wore a tan duster that nearly brushed the floor in a way that was entirely dashing. He had a faded red bandanna tied around his neck and some kind of flat-brimmed gaucho-style hat that appeared to have seen better days. The whole look was topped off with the shadow on his square jaw of what had to be the sexiest two days' growth of beard Lara had ever seen.

He looked thoroughly disreputable. Thoroughly dangerous.

It had been a week since the episode in her bedroom, when she'd decided she must, as Connor was doing, move on with her life, although she hadn't a clue as to how. Her conversation just now with her aunt, however, gave her an inkling that it wasn't going to be so easy as merely setting her mind to the task. For how was she to do that without resolving that past—or more specifically, the incident she and Connor shared in their fathers' pasts that had affected her entire life?

Thank goodness he mistook the nature of her stare. "You don't get who I am, do you?"

She shook her head dumbly.

He gave an exaggerated sigh of exasperation before he sauntered toward her with a jingle of spurs, flicking back the sides of the duster to expose the gunbelt slung low on his lean hips.

"Are you gonna pull those pistols," he said, stopping in front of her, in a dead-on imitation of Clint Eastwood, "or whistle Dixie?"

Then he cocked an imaginary six-shooter in a way that certainly made her want to surrender without a fight.

Lara mustered a smile. "I'm thinking you're Clint Eastwood, but in which part fails me."

"The Outlaw Josey Wales," he confirmed, beaming at her, his smile distracting her again. Those dimples of his were so much deeper than she remembered.

Lara cleared her throat. "Yes. Yes, of course," she lied.

"I guess it *is* hard to tell," Connor admitted. "I thought it best to leave out the stub of a cigar clamped between my teeth, and real six-shooters." A sobering shadow like the one she'd seen before crossed his handsome features. "I didn't think either prop would exactly set an example for the kids."

"Oh, that's right." She gestured around her with the candy bowl. "I understand you're the one responsible for all this?"

"You don't know? I phoned here a few hours ago and asked Bev to call over to the elementary school, let the teachers all know the kids were welcome to come here after they got out for the day for sort of a Halloween open house. I thought it might be a good opportunity to have parents and children down here to get acquainted with you as the new P.A. in town. Having a familiarity with you is going to be important to everyone's learning to trust you for their health care."

"Really?" Pleasure blossomed within Lara's chest. What a thoughtful gesture! How comfortable people felt with her *would* be important to her effectiveness. "Well, I only wish I'd known sooner. I'd have worn a costume, too. Maybe made up a display of health care tips for parents."

He apparently mistook her disappointment for pique. "I only thought of the party this afternoon when I stopped in Bridgewater on an errand and noticed the stores along Main Street were having trick-or-treat for kids after school." His mouth turned down. "Sorry for the short notice. I guess I didn't think you'd have had ideas for the party, too."

"Oh, no, Connor. No." Lara impulsively reached a hand out to him, catching herself before she touched him. "There's no need to apologize. It was…well, it was wonderful of you to think of doing this at all. See how well your idea's working?"

They both glanced around. Children continued to arrive dressed in every kind of costume, from a slew of Harry Potters to a bevy of fairy princesses. They crowded around Frannie, who was demonstrating a remarkable talent for fashioning balloon animals. In another corner Bev, who'd returned a few minutes before, dressed as a farmer in a straw hat and an oversize pair of what had to be her husband's overalls, was supervising the apple-bobbing contest, while parents sipped hot cider and bade their children not to be too greedy, too loud or too rambunctious.

Lara noticed, too, that Connor's presence gave several people pause, although a few young boys and girls were taking in his out-lawish costume with admiration.

Of course, there were exceptions. He dropped to his haunches in front of a four-year-old girl dressed as a sunflower, her chubby face surrounded by an aura of yellow petals.

"And what's your name, sweetheart?" he asked with that devastating smile, which was obviously lost on the child. She screamed and burst into tears.

"Hey now, there's no reason to cry," Connor said in an intimate tone that sent a heated shiver through Lara. He reached into the inside breast pocket of his duster and pulled out a sucker. "I was just gonna ask what trick you've worked up to earn treats today."

The youngster's mother, who'd been looking on with a concerned expression that mirrored her daughter's, gave the child a slight nudge. "Be nice to Mr. Brody here, honey, and tell him the joke you learned."

The child sniffed mightily, clutched the plastic orange pumpkin containing her candy with both chubby hands, then said in a trembling voice, "Why'd the man frow the c-clock out the window?"

Scratching his chin, Connor pondered the conundrum. "Gosh, I don't have a clue. Why?"

"He...he wanted to see time fly!" the girl said triumphantly.

Connor laughed, that oh-so-attractive rumble that came up from his chest. "You got me there, darlin'." He held out the lollipop and she took it with a shy, watery smile.

Chock up one more convert to the Connor Brody Fan Club.

Yes, he seemed to take in stride the askance looks he was receiving from some parents as he introduced himself, Lara noticed. As for herself, word had gotten around how she had helped Bobby Dayton, and she was asked about herself in that friendly yet purposeful way Texans size others up.

When she revealed that she was Griff Corbin's cousin, an elderly woman introduced to Lara as Alma Butters and sporting a silver beehive that truly defined "big hair" piped up, "Of course, that's where I remember your name from! Your family lived in that cute two-story frame house out on the edge of town just this side of the railroad tracks, didn't you?"

"Yes," Lara answered tersely, hoping the woman wouldn't pursue the subject. She might as well have expected rain to fall upward.

"I remember your daddy worked on that house day and night, it seemed," Alma continued, obviously warming to her topic. "Why, you didn't pass by there without seein' him up on a ladder just pounding away with a hammer like a man possessed." She clasped Lara's wrist in confidence. "You can be sure the place hasn't been so well tended since."

"I'm sure it hasn't," Lara murmured, a note of closure in her voice that was for naught.

"How'd your family fare after you left Bridgewater, anyway? Last Web Corbin would say was your daddy'd left Tanglewood and gone north to take a job and get settled 'fore your mama and you moved up to be with him."

Forget discretion, Lara thought. Nearby, Connor had obviously picked up on the conversation and was listening avidly while trying to seem not to listen at all. It would have been funny had Lara not been desperate that he find out no more about her family's history.

And desperate times called for desperate measures. She grabbed the other woman's forearm and pulled her aside. "Sorry to interrupt, Mrs. Butters, but you've obviously been a resident of this area for many years?"

"All my life," Alma averred.

"Excellent." Lara bent closer, taking Alma into *her* confidence. "I'd like to start an initiative to provide education to menopausal and postmenopausal women in the community. The thing is, I really need someone to lead the project whom people know and trust. Someone like you."

"Me!" Alma exclaimed, her hand fluttering to needlessly smooth the indestructible beehive. "Why, I'd be honored! I'm always telling people they need to take better care of themselves."

"I'm sure you are," Lara murmured. "So, if you wouldn't mind coming by the clinic tomorrow so we can have a real talk?"

"Not at all, not at all." And Alma turned to find a repository for this latest bit of news.

She was distracted, as was everyone else in the room, by the arrival of a striking redhead who, catching sight of Connor, gave an exclamation of delight and fairly flung herself into his arms.

He hugged her back with relish, releasing her with a grin as she rabbit-punched him in the chest.

"What have you been doin' with yourself, you skunk?" she said fondly. "We haven't seen you in weeks, ever since you hired Griff to look after Tanglewood." Her head wagged back and forth reproachfully. "Obviously, you're just too important to mingle with us anymore, you king of the cattle ranchers."

"Oh, yeah, that's me all over," Connor said, grinning.

"That's Addie Gentry, in case you were wondering," Alma said sotto voce into Lara's ear with the air of a spy delivering state secrets. "The two of 'em were engaged up till a year ago. T'were somethin' of a scandal when she broke it off. Brodys don't tend to take that kind of news well, if you know what I mean."

"I'm sure I don't," Lara said coolly. But she couldn't deny it—jealousy pricked her at the obvious affection he had for this woman.

And just what did Lara have to be jealous about? Nothing! But she definitely didn't like the thought of Connor Brody carrying a torch for the woman he had once loved enough to ask her to marry him.

They both noticed her standing to one side, her lips turned upward in what she felt sure was a stiff and unbecoming smile.

"And you must be Lara!" the redhead exclaimed as she ushered a handsome, dark-haired boy toward Lara. "Sorry we're late. I'm Addie, and this here's Jace, my son. As you can see, I didn't have time to make him a Halloween costume, crowning me Worst

Mother Ever, I'm sure. It's just that we've been up to our belt buckles tryin' to get the herd ready for market next week."

All of this was delivered rapid-fire and without the least affectation, making Lara decide then and there that she liked this woman, no matter what her history was with Connor.

Lara shook her hand heartily. "It's a pleasure to meet you."

"And I've been dying to meet *you.*" Addie pushed back one side of the suede Western jacket she wore to reveal what was to Lara's practiced eye an advanced pregnancy. "I've been goin' into Houston to see my doctor there for my checkups. But both my husband and I would feel a whole lot better 'bout being so far away from the hospital if we knew you could handle an emergency, should it come up." Her pretty face was tinged with concern.

"I certainly can," Lara assured her. "Why don't you make an appointment to come in and see me next week and we'll talk about some of your options."

"Bring that husband of yours along, too," Connor added. He gave Lara a wink of encouragement that made her blush despite her every prayer that she wouldn't. She hoped no one would notice. "It might ease his mind as well to know you're in Lara's good hands."

Addie's features cleared. "That would be great."

Under cover of hiding her pinkened face, Lara turned to the boy at her side. "And you're welcome to come, too, Jace."

The boy's eyebrows puckered in doubt, lifting the brim of his cowboy hat a fraction of an inch. "Maybe. But like Mama said, we got to get that herd ready, and if she and Daddy come to town, they'll need someone to stay and keep an eye on things."

He was so serious, Lara had to struggle to hide her smile. Cocking her head to one side, she observed, "I'd say you don't need a Halloween costume, Jace. Looks to me you've got being a rancher down pat."

The boy's green-gold eyes lit up. "That's 'cause I'm a Larrabie," he confirmed.

"Larrabie. Where have I heard that name before?" she asked before thinking. A hush fell over the room, and it was only then that Lara realized the four of them had an audience.

From the corner of her eye she caught the shadow, now familiar to her, that passed over Connor's features.

Of course. How could she have forgotten? Larrabie had been the name of the man Griff told her Mick Brody had been convicted of killing.

Lara realized that Addie must have noticed as well the uneasiness—no, the downright fear—that pervaded the room.

"Connor must have mentioned Deke to you, that's where you heard it," the redhead said with cool calm. But Lara could tell she was scared. Scared for Connor. This was not what he needed, to have that incident be exhumed at this moment, when he was trying to help Lara get people familiar with her and trust her.

"Well," she said. Then, clearing her throat, she repeated more strongly, "Well, Addie. Jace. Please help yourself to punch and goodies. Connor arranged for all this, you know, so people could meet me. You knew, didn't you, that Connor brought me to Bridgewater, at his own expense, to run this clinic? Without him, I wouldn't have this chance to serve you and your children, and provide you with the best health care that can be afforded. I don't know but that Connor Brody's just about the best friend this town's had in a long time!"

This rousing endorsement Lara delivered to the group at large. Admittedly, she'd done so with a heavy hand. Still, she could see it had a limited effect. There were as many coldly skeptical faces as there were contemplative ones. And she understood better than ever the Catch-22 Connor operated under: even though her presence here was his doing, *his* presence here was a liability to that cause.

Her eyes settled back on Addie, whose own eyes were pensive, and Lara got the strangest sense that, rather than Connor, *she* was the object of Addie's doubt.

Did Addie know about what had happened between Mick Brody and Lara's father? Something told her that she didn't. There was *something* in her gaze, however, that was knowing in the way that women have.

Then Lara was drawn to look at Connor. And oh, what she saw shining in those deep brown eyes! His gratitude to her, first, for standing up for him. But there was something more there, too…a recognition of her effort to bring the townspeople closer to forgiving and forgetting, to accepting a man in his own right.

And not holding the sins of his father against him.

So *was* that what she'd been trying to convey?

She couldn't say, not even now. How could she, though, when she barely knew Connor other than as the son of Mick Brody?

She felt a hand on her elbow, and Lara turned blindly to find her aunt at her side.

"It's just about time for the costume contest, and seein' as how it's mighty expensive to look this cheap, I aim to win the fifty dollar first prize Connor's put up!" she announced in her perkiest Dolly voice.

But her eyes, as they rested on Lara, were also knowing, making Lara wonder what it was she still missed about the situation involving Bridgewater and Connor. And herself.

Chapter Five

"Well, Miss Dearborn, I'd have to say your get-acquainted party did the trick," Connor said, gazing up at Lara, who was perched on the steps of a ladder, tugging at the tape holding the crepe paper to the ceiling.

She handed the streamers down to him to be rolled into a ball. "If it did, it's all due to you, Mr. Wales. Or is it Mr. Outlaw?"

With a slow smile, he touched a fingertip to the brim of his hat, looking at her from beneath it in a way that nearly had her clutching the ladder for balance. "I answer to both, ma'am," he drawled.

She blushed, her face heating up with soldering gun intensity. Clearly, he was still appreciative of the vignette of prairie justice that had taken place, courtesy of one Lara Dearborn. And she was still stirred up by the look he had given her afterward as a result.

Fortunately, Connor had seemed determined not to let that brief pall spoil the mood of the party, and had soon gotten the children, if not all their parents, involved in judging the best costume of the day. The winner had actually been a boy dressed up as Elvis in the Vegas years, complete with oversize black pompadour. Frannie had done her bit to liven things up by pretending to be Dolly in the throes of jealousy about who looked best in their spandex pantsuit.

"So you're going to be talkin' with Addie about what options she has for when she delivers?" Connor asked, drawing Lara back to the present.

"Yes. I've been trained in delivery techniques. I'm not an OB, and I don't have the advantage of a fully equipped birthing room, but in an emergency, I can provide medical care." She worried her bottom lip with her teeth. "Since Doc Becker retired, it's probably been awfully scary for all the women around here, to be so far from a real doctor and hospital when they're pregnant."

"No doubt. As I understand it, a lot of women used him as their primary doctor for their pregnancy, and not as a backup to one in Houston. With the nearest hospital thirty-five miles away, he no doubt had to deliver a few babies right here at the clinic in a pinch."

Connor paused, then said softly, "In any case, I'm glad you'll be here for Addie."

Lara concentrated on folding the Halloween banner she'd taken down into neat squares so it would fit back into its plastic package. "She seems to be very special to you," she commented.

"You could say that." He helped her climb down from the ladder, then folded it and set it near the door to be taken back to Frannie's. "I owe a lot to her and Deke, her husband. Fact is, I don't know how I'd've made it these past months without their ranching help—and their friendship. Deke's a helluva good cowboy. He and Addie are about as well matched as two people can be."

He gave a short laugh. "Believe it or not, she and I were fixin' to get married when he came back on the scene to claim her and the son they'd had together. Of course, at the time I thought it was about the worst thing that could happen. But as you can see, it all turned out for the best."

"Oh!" Lara hoped he didn't notice the relief in that one word, but it was obvious he held not one iota of rancor against anyone, or regret for what had happened.

She really ought to take a page from his book, if it were at all possible to do so.

Deciding she must come clean about at least one matter, Lara took a deep breath. "I want to apologize, Connor, for my slip this afternoon. Really, I didn't mean to make anyone uncomfortable by mentioning the Larrabies."

"Apologize for what? You didn't say anything people weren't thinking. And you sure made up for it." He came over to the couch, where she had taken a seat next to the box in which they were storing the decorations for next year, and sat down beside her. "I meant to thank you for that."

His voice had dropped to an intimate rumble that made her break out in a cold sweat.

Lara gave a rueful laugh. "Yes, well, it wouldn't have been needed if I hadn't brought up the Larrabie name."

He reached for the unused black and orange balloons she'd spilled on the floor in front of her, and stuffed them into their plastic package. "Lara. Addie and Jace *are* Larrabies, in the flesh. If anything, their presence here made more of a statement than anything you might have said."

"Yes, but…some things are better left unsaid, if they're to be put behind by everyone for good."

She dropped her chin, unable to look him in the eye, and pretended to take up a renewed quest to ensure the wires to the pumpkin lights were tangle-free.

From beside her, Connor asked quietly, "Lara...did your father work at Tanglewood?"

Oh, this was one subject that was definitely better left untouched. "Yes. A l-long, long time ago, and not for a great length of time, as I remember."

"Did he...did he ever talk about, you know, what it was like to work for my dad?" From the corner of her eye, Lara saw Connor lean forward, elbows on his knees and hands clasped between them. "I mean, I've heard tell from some folks what Dad was like back then, after...well, I think after his and my mother's marriage went sour. I've heard that it laid him low—humbled him and made him more tolerant, at least for a while. Although I think he's always had a knack for rubbing people both the wrong way and the right way at the same time."

Connor slanted her a sideways glance. "But I'd like to know what your daddy might've thought of him."

He had an obvious need to know, even if it wasn't the best news, if his father had any redeeming qualities among the bad ones. As Connor talked, Lara had lifted her chin to gaze at his profile—that strong, cleanly cut jaw, the finely drawn mouth. And of course, those mercurial dimples, which could convey both mirth and torment by their depth and slant.

"Dad never spoke of Tanglewood or your father," she answered truthfully. "Not to me, at least."

Casting his gaze at the floor between the toes of his boots, Connor gave a sigh and nodded shortly. "I guess I thought he might have—from the way you reacted to finding out my name when we first met." He raised his head and looked her straight in the eye. "Like my family had done yours a personal wrong. Did we?"

Lara stared back at him. She couldn't lie to him, yet something told her that to tell the whole truth would be devastating to Connor. And to her, too. It was too personal a hurt, and she did not want to be in a position of such vulnerability with this man she still knew so little about.

"I—I'm sorry for that reaction, Connor." Ashamed of herself for not answering his question, Lara automatically reached out, meaning once again to set her hand on his, before she caught herself. She'd have had to be a fool to think he didn't notice.

She shook her head helplessly, unable—or actually unwilling—to explain. "I'm sorry."

"Sorry for what? It was probably just my imagination." He shrugged, but she could tell he was still bothered. "Then I guess my question is, what *did* happen?"

"Happen?" she parroted inanely.

"Between us."

His hand covered hers, his fingers curling around hers to brush her palm. "It seemed to me, for a few minutes there when we first met, that we shared...I don't know. Something special. I thought I'd imagined it, but then I felt it today, too. Am I wrong?"

Pulling away from him, she rose, taking a half-dozen aimless steps away from him. She couldn't let him see that truth in her eyes. Not yet.

"Lara," he said from behind her, his voice pitched low and weakening her resolve. "Just talk to me, won't you?"

Taking a deep breath, she blurted out before she lost her nerve, "You have to understand something about me, Connor. I—I have this...thing I do, when I'm getting to know someone—"

"Someone?"

"All right, I mean men." She hugged herself, her fingers digging into her upper arms as if it were freezing in the room. "Trust doesn't come automatically to me. It never has. And when it comes to trusting m-men— well, I don't know if it ever will. Not…completely."

There. It was out. She wondered how he would react to her revelation. Like the others? For when it had gotten to this point in a relationship in the past, and she'd either revealed her doubt or made it pretty clear that's where she stood, the men she'd been seeing had invariably opted out.

A few, though, had professed that it didn't make a difference. But in the end, it had. Sooner or later, they'd realized that there wasn't much chance of having a truly fulfilling relationship with a woman who was unable to let herself be vulnerable. To be able to be hurt or disappointed in the way that human beings are destined to hurt one another, to acknowledge the wound, and yet go on loving.

And of course, such an issue always had the effect, desired or otherwise, of ending her involvement.

Lara pressed her lips together. She didn't think it the best sign in the world that she'd made this speech to Connor now. After all, they didn't have anything that could be remotely construed as a relationship. But never before had she felt her equilibrium so threatened.

Then again, never before had she cared that a man understand her completely.

"I'm sure that makes me seem pretty uptight." She couldn't keep the defensiveness out of her voice.

"It might," Connor said, "if I didn't hold the same opinion, that trust *shouldn't* come automatically, or quickly, or easily."

She turned to face him. "You don't?"

He stood. "No. These things take time." He shrugged, giving her a clue that perhaps he had some secrets to reveal, as well. "Sometimes I think I go the opposite route and trust too much, too soon. And talk about causin' a peck of trouble, not just for me but for others."

She had to ask. "You mean...with Addie?"

"I mean with my dad." He shook his head ruefully. "Up until a few years ago, the only relationship I had with him was a couple of holidays a year and a month in the summer at Tanglewood. I knew firsthand he could be crotchety and even surly sometimes, but I figured that was just his way."

Connor flicked back the edges of his duster, hooking his thumbs over the top of his gunbelt in a thoughtful stance. "Mom never said a bad word about him in all the years after their divorce, and I was led to believe incompatibility had been the reason for their breakup."

Lara had to ask. "It wasn't?"

"No." He took a deep breath. "The rumors about Mick Brody, the fear people have of him? I'm afraid most of it's justified, Lara. And not just because it was discovered years after the fact that he was responsible for the death of D. K. Larrabie. When I came to Tanglewood a few years ago to learn the ropes, so to speak, so I could take over the ranch, it took me a while, but I eventually caught on to how Dad's always been pretty ruthless. Successful, but ruthless. And once I realized that, I knew that wasn't the kind of rancher I wanted to be. Not the kind of man I wanted to be, either."

Absently, he rubbed the engraved buckle of his gunbelt with the edge of his thumb. "It was the hardest thing I've ever done, turnin' Dad over to the authorities. But even when he was yelling at me how I was no son of his, I...I could see real clearly that that wasn't the man that he wanted to be, either. He was at the mercy of inclinations that were about as destructive as you could get. And while that doesn't absolve him, it does make it easier to understand him. To feel some compassion for him. And to forgive him."

She could not tear her eyes from Connor's, so stunned was she by his words and the strength of emotion in the deep, dark brown depths. She was so caught up in the spell he'd cast, she didn't even realize he'd moved her to tears until he asked, "Why are you cryin', Lara?"

"Because!" she said fiercely. With shaking fingers, she wiped away the moisture on her cheeks. "For the disappointment you must have endured, must still be enduring, that Mick isn't the father you deserve." Her voice, she realized, shook with anger. "Doesn't it make you angry that he wasn't there for you?"

"I guess it does sometimes, when I'm feelin' particularly down about things. But he is what he is. And part of what he is, for better or worse, is my dad."

For better or worse. They were words exchanged not in a vow between parent and child, but between man and wife. *In sickness and in health.*

Till death do us part.

"I think," she said in a low voice, "that you must be a better person than I am, b-being able to forgive so easily."

He lifted her chin so she had to look him in the eye once again. "Oh, it's not easy at all," he murmured, "just like trustin' doesn't come easy for you." His gaze dropped to her mouth. "But that's all right...all right with me...."

His liquid brown eyes grew even darker, and he leaned toward her. And kissed her.

It was different than the last time—it had to be, given that she knew now who he was. And yet, strangely—miraculously—it was the same. His mouth was as gentle, letting her get used to his touch, letting her get used to letting go, as she so often dreamed of doing in those daydreams she had, where she was able to give herself over to trusting a man.

As she so often dreamed of—and so feared. Because the pain would be unendurable when he went away.

I've come to tell you he's left you, Pauline.

Left? Wh-what can you mean, Mick?

Dooley—he bought a one-way ticket on a bus headed west just this afternoon. I saw him get on it myself. And you may as well know the truth—I'm the one responsible for his leavin'.

But...he couldn't have gone! Things were gettin' better. He told me so!

Yeah, well, things were better till he messed up good today, caused an accident with my best cow pony so's I had to put the animal down. I was so gol-durned mad I lit into him, told him everyone would be better off if he'd just disappear.

No. No! Oh, how could you? You knew what frame of mind he's been in! You couldn't've had the common decency to temper your words, not in the least? I mean, Dooley even told me you and he had gotten to be friends—

Damn it, Pauline, I did what I had to do! And the best thing you can do for yourself and your little girl is forget about him! He's gone! And he's never comin' back.

Lara drew back, panic assaulting her. How could she? How could she even begin to trust the man whose father was responsible for the destruction of hers?

Grabbing on to that notion, Lara lashed out rashly. "Was this part of the plan, too?" she asked.

Connor frowned in confusion. "Plan?"

She took a step away from him, out of his reach and out of the sphere of his influence on her. "You're obviously out to court the town, even the whole county. Why not the new P.A., as well, who'll be gaining everyone's trust?"

She flung her arm out, indicating the whole of the waiting room, which only an hour before had been filled with happy, chattering children enjoying an afternoon of fun—and parents who wanted only the best for those children—courtesy of Connor.

"Tell me you didn't plan this Halloween party not to help people in getting to know me, but as yet another attempt to build up *your* reputation in Bridgewater as the great and wonderful Connor Brody!"

CONNOR HAD TO give himself credit for spotting a little sooner than before the fear in her eyes. It had less to do with him specifically than with that other issue boiling within her, he suspected.

That wasn't to say that seeing her beautiful gray eyes turn angry and wary didn't carve a mile-deep gash in his spirit. In fact, experiencing Lara's irrationality where he was concerned fairly ate him up, even knowing this time that her radical reaction didn't entirely have to do with him being a Brody.

Which meant it had to do with him being just him.

One thing her reaction did tell him, loud and clear, was that she was not exaggerating in the least when she said she had a problem learning to trust. It would take some intensive patience and care to bring her past that.

And the number one question was, was he the man to do it?

Actually, the ultimate question was why the hell did he care so much? Really, *that* was the one that didn't bear asking. Heaven knew he'd done a bang-up job over the past week of convincing himself he didn't give a hoot about Lara Dearborn, especially after the way she had gazed at him in what had been dangerously close to pity that evening in her bedroom as she held those remarkable mementos of her hero father.

Hadn't Connor just admitted, though, that he knew what it was like to have compassion for someone—because what was compassion but just a polite way of saying pity? And while either of those might lead to understanding and hopefully to forgiving, the last thing on God's green earth he wanted from Lara was pity for being Mick Brody's son. He'd rather have her fear!

He stared down into those angry, anxious gray eyes that only moments before had been melting, the lips that still glistened from his kiss. So should he continue to try with her, continue to hang his heart out there on a string to yet again let a woman come and take a whack at it as if it was a full-to-bursting piñata? Why not? Hadn't he already been doing that on a certain level with the people of Bridgewater—turning the other cheek when he was given the sort of back-handed compliments that Russ Dayton had come up with? Certainly, Connor conceded Lara's point that much of the time his motive for helping people in town *was* to try, with the best of intentions, to make up for the wrongs his father had committed.

And in the case of this Halloween party, she was technically right. He had to admit it. Sure, he'd been hoping to help her; his intentions there were true. But in the back of his mind he'd also hoped she'd see him as the cowboy hero who would save the town before riding into the sunset.

Clint Eastwood, however, he was not. And never would be.

"So this party was all about me, you're saying." Connor again closed the distance between them, flinching inwardly when he saw the fear return to her eyes.

Yet she stood up to him, despite the very real threat he seemed to pose to her. "Can you honestly tell me you didn't do this to impress the people of Bridgewater?" she demanded.

No! It was on the tip of his tongue to say that. *If anything, it was to impress you.* But what good would it do?

"I guess you're gonna believe, just like everyone else in this town, what you're gonna believe," he said instead. "And my actions be damned."

He turned his back to her and headed for the door, which, to his irritation, was stuck and took a good three tries to yank open, improving his mood not a whit.

He pivoted, hand gripping the brass door-knob so hard he heard the joints on two fingers crack.

"Well, you're on your own now, Lara," he said in parting, meaning more than the sticky door. "You'll sink or swim under your own power—just like I'm doin'."

WHENEVER LIFE AND love got a little too much for her, Lara did what any red-blooded American woman would do, and declared Saturday night testosterone-free. Women only, no men allowed.

That meant renting chick flicks at the video store, and tonight that included some of her favorites: *Thelma and Louise, Fried Green Tomatoes* and *Like Water for Chocolate.* Chocolate itself was an obvious staple, as were the most comfy, unsexy pajamas that could be found in the land.

Standing before the full-length mirror in her bedroom, Lara gazed with satisfaction at her sleepwear—a pair of plaid flannel pa-

"I was down at the Diamond Tap," he explained in gasps. "Stopped by there on my way back from Houston to pick up a chicken-fried steak, when I heard...I heard a couple of women talkin' to the waitress about this family out on the west side of town that's got two kids who're sick."

He paused, not for effect, but his next words nevertheless made an impact. "If they don't have rheumatic fever, then they're well on their way to getting it, from what these women said."

"No!" Lara said in dismay. "I mean, I know there's been a bout of strep throat making its way around the school—I've probably seen a half-dozen kids with it in the past week and a half." She shook her head. "So why didn't the parents bring the children in to see me? Strep is a very obvious illness to diagnose and easy to treat with antibiotics!"

"I don't know." He gazed at her sharply. "But I think it'd be best to get over there tonight and see what can be done, if you don't mind."

She gazed up at him in surprise. "Of course I don't mind! Why would I?"

"Because I'm coming with you. Who knows what the kids might need or what state the parents'll be in themselves?" Reaching up, he grasped his black Stetson by the crown, re-settling it firmly a notch farther down on his brow. "You'll need some help, and that means from me. Given how we didn't exactly part on the best of terms last time we talked, you might have some objection to that."

Without batting a lash, Lara replied briskly, "I couldn't care less if you were Attila the Hun in the flesh. We have two sick children who need help from any quarter they can get it right now."

To her surprise, one side of his mouth turned up in a slow smile of admiration. "I'll say this, you're a real pro, Lara."

Her flush of pleasure was pushed a good twenty degrees hotter by his gaze slowly sliding down the length of her, making Lara realize she wore a thin T-shirt and no bra. Then his eyes lit on the Miss Piggy slippers. He raised his eyebrows in inquiry.

"Don't ask," she begged. "It's a woman thing."

"I didn't say a word," he drawled.

"Just give me a minute to throw on a jacket and put on proper shoes. I'll need to stop by the clinic to pick up some supplies, too."

"I'll wait in the pickup," Connor said from behind her, for she was already on her way down the hall to her bedroom.

Ten minutes later, Lara was sitting next to Connor as he sped through town toward the clinic. Once there, she took but a minute to collect a bag with the instruments and medications she knew she'd need.

"Do you know where the family lives?" she asked as he made a U-turn once she'd climbed back into his truck.

"It's out on Third Avenue, the waitress at the tap said. I'm pretty sure I can find it." He looked terribly intent, his strong features illuminated in the green glow of the truck's dashboard lights, and she was suddenly glad to see him again. To be working with him and not against him.

"Just to give you a heads-up," he said after a few moments. "People around here aren't backward, by any means. But for whatever reason, I think that these parents aren't going to welcome us showin' up at their door and telling them what they need to be doing to look after their kids' health properly. If they had a lot of faith in medicine, they'd have brought the youngsters into the clinic or taken them to another doctor long ago. You know?"

"I see what you mean." Lara shifted the bag on her lap. Within it were the tools to diagnose and treat many ills. Within her was the knowledge to make those diagnoses. But just like everything else in life, people had to either pick up the tools available to them or accept the help that came their way, in order for either to be of any use.

"We'll just have to do the best we can," she said.

Connor gave her a quick glance that even in the dim light seemed filled with meaning. "Yes."

Turning onto Third Avenue, he leaned forward, squinting at the houses set back from the street.

"What's the address?" Lara asked.

"Don't know. It's supposed to be the last one before you cross the railroad tracks."

She frowned. The last house before the railroad tracks? Why did that ring a bell with her?

She realized why just as Connor announced, "Here it is." He turned the truck into the gravel drive and pulled up next to a rather worse-for-wear two-story frame house.

Lara could only sit there and stare out the window at the familiar structure. The big cedar on the west side was gone. Someone had taken down the dark green shutters, making the home's plain white facade look more stark than usual.

But it was the window centered within the

gable on the second floor that drew Lara's gaze. The view from it she knew like her own face in a mirror. She had sat before it so many times, gazing out at the far-off horizon, while the voices of her parents carried the urgency of their situation up to her from below.

Dooley, I'm beggin' you. Just...stay a little longer, won't you? That couldn't hurt, could it?

Could it, Pauline? I already feel like a man half-dead inside, with the other half bein' eaten away bit by bit. You're right— how could that hurt any more than it already does?

"Lara?"

She turned to find Connor leaning on the open door and peering into the cab at her. "Is there something wrong?" he asked.

"Wrong? What could be wrong?" she said, only then realizing how snappish she'd sounded.

"I'm only askin'," he said stiffly.

She stared at him, desperately trying to form some evasive answer. But she couldn't do it. Already she could see that her preoccupation had brought back the distance between them. And what had he told her the last time he saw her? That she was on her own. She'd have to sink or swim without his help.

But she couldn't do it. She couldn't go into that house and do her best to treat those children—not with any kind of distance between her and the man she would need to count on to help her.

"I'm sorry, Connor," she said. She put her hand to her forehead and realized it was damp with nervous perspiration. "You see, this is the house I lived in before I left Bridgewater twenty years ago."

He glanced quickly toward the house, then back to her quizzically. "Yeah, you already told me your family moved up to Dallas."

"No, it wasn't my family. It was only Mom and I."

Lara turned her head to stare at the gabled window again. "My father was already long gone."

Chapter Six

"Whaddaya want?"

Connor was surprised to see that the man who came to the back door in response to his knock was much older than he'd expected, a good sixty years old if he was a day. For some reason, Connor had imagined these parents must be very young. Too young to know better.

But he recognized this man, had seen him at Kearney's Tack and Feed Store on Main Street. He drove a truck for one of the cattle supply companies. Roy McDuffy was his name. It was embroidered above the breast pocket of the light blue shirt he wore.

"We understand you have a couple of sick children here," Lara told the man gently. She indicated the doctor's bag she held. "I'm a physician's assistant. We've come to help."

He peered at her suspiciously. "You're the

one that's new to Doc Becker's clinic, ain't you?"

"Why yes, I am," she said. "Perhaps you know Russ Dayton, whose boy I treated a month or so ago?"

Connor understood why she brought up the Dayton boy—to provide what amounted to credentials as to her competence.

Not that it seemed to do any good. "Can't say as I do," McDuffy said curtly. He lifted the newspaper he held, indicating the road behind them. "Well, I appreciate your good intentions, but we're doin' just fine. Now if y'all don't mind—"

"I'm afraid we can't leave," Connor said firmly, pressing his palm against the door as McDuffy began to shut it. "If you'll just let Lara take a look at the children, I'm sure she can help keep them from getting any sicker."

"Oh, you're *sure,* are ya?" he challenged. He took a step closer to both of them, and Connor put a protective arm around Lara's shoulders, challenge in his own gaze as he stared the man down.

McDuffy met his eyes unflinchingly. "Don't think I don't know who you are, Brody. And I know for damn certain we don't need *your* help here—"

"Let them in, Roy."

A pale, thin woman with a cap of graying hair stood at the threshold of the kitchen, a white basin tucked against her side.

"June…" Roy said, the word a warning.

She gave her husband a look that was half pleading, half implacable.

"Let them in," she repeated. "I can't get Annie's fever to break, and Jessie's joints are achin' so much she can't get comfortable." Her voice broke. "She just keeps thrashin' around, sayin' 'Granny, make it stop hurting.'"

Connor could see McDuffy's Adam's apple bob in his throat. He bent his head. "All right then," he said fiercely, his voice so low Connor could barely hear him. "I'm not a man to deny my grandbabies real help if it's to be had."

Within an instant, Lara had brushed past him through the door, Connor following close behind. For a moment, he thought the man might make a move to block his way, but Connor wasn't about to wait around and give him that chance.

The children were upstairs in a gabled room that had originally been an attic. Two little girls, one about ten and the other only about five, Connor guessed, lay in twin beds on either side of the window, their breathing labored and irregular.

He watched Lara pause at the doorway, and he got the strangest sensation that she was shocked, not by the children's condition, but by the room itself.

Of course. This had to have been her bedroom when she lived here. What had she meant about just her mother and her leaving here twenty years before? Where had her father gone? From what he'd overheard Alma Butters say at the Halloween open house, Lara's father had left to take a job in north Texas and get settled there before his wife and daughter joined him.

But Lara had indicated that her father had left town long before she and her mother did, implying that he had left the two of them.

Unable to prevent himself from offering her comfort, Connor felt for Lara's hand and squeezed it in support. She did not return the gesture.

In fact, whatever memory had stopped Lara at the doorway apparently passed quickly, for in the next moment she was across the floor and at the bedside of the younger child, all-business.

"What's your name, sweetheart?" she asked gently, indicating that Connor should set her bag at the end of the bed. He did so, standing back as she delved within it for her stethoscope.

"Annie," the girl answered through chapped, cracking lips. "Annie Marie Buckley, I mean."

"It's nice to meet you, Annie Marie Buckley."

The little girl stared up at her with weary eyes, her dark hair plastered to her scalp and her cheeks flushed with fever.

"Are you an angel?" she asked in a timorous voice.

"No," Lara said with a low chuckle, pressing the scope to the small chest. "I'm Lara, and I've come to help you and your sister get better. Can you take in a big breath for me?"

The child sucked in a ragged breath that made her cough weakly. "That sounds to me like what an angel does, don't it to you?"

Lara laughed softly. "I guess it could."

Connor could see how the child got that impression. The light from the bedside lamp cast a warm glow upon Lara, making her shiny blond hair gleam like an aura around her face, which wore an expression of such kindness, such compassion, it seemed angelic.

He had to admit it. Even in a bomber jacket and a pair of plaid pajama bottoms, and without a speck of makeup on, she indeed looked every inch an angel of mercy.

And as desirable to him as ever.

He'd suffered quite a few bouts of remorse for sounding off to her at their last meeting. She'd definitely hit a sore spot with him. And while she'd had no right to say what she did to him, she had also warned him of how hard it was for her to trust men—and he'd essentially ignored that, so caught up was he in wanting to kiss her.

Maybe she had good reason to be wary of him, he thought, clenching his teeth in self-reproach.

"Now, this is going to feel kind of icky," Lara was saying. She'd taken out a culture stick and, asking Annie to open wide, reached in to swab the back of the girl's throat.

Annie gagged and coughed. "Ugh!" she proclaimed once Lara had withdrawn the stick and swiped it across a glass slide.

"That was the worst part of the exam," she told the youngster. "We're all done. You did great."

"Am I gonna be okay?" Annie asked, fear in her high voice.

Lara soothed the hair back from the child's forehead. "You're going to be fine, Annie. I promise."

Mrs. McDuffy stepped forward from the doorway, where she and Roy had been standing in tense silence. "What about Jessie? She's sick, too."

"Yes, let's have a look at Jessie now."

Lara shifted to the other girl's bed. There was no question that the older of the two children would not be as easily placated as the younger had been.

"Are we gonna die?" she asked in a stage whisper, shooting a furtive glance at her sister.

"Not if I have anything to say about it," Lara said staunchly as she began to examine her. "Why would you think you might, Jessie?"

"It's just…" The girl turned her head on the pillow, staring at the wall for a moment. Then she said in a soft voice, "It's just that I'm worried about Granny and Papa. They cain't take no more people leavin' 'em."

Connor heard Lara's soft gasp, but not her response, as the girls' grandmother said beside him, "She means their mama, our daughter. She lit out for the West Coast when Annie here weren't no more than a peanut."

His heart squeezed in empathy for what Jessie's words must have churned up inside of Lara. She had already been buffeted by more than a few blows this evening, he knew.

He turned his head to look at the older woman—hadn't McDuffy called her June?—whose gaze was fixed upon Lara as she ministered to her granddaughter. "Roy run their daddy off long 'fore then," she was saying, and made a face of disgust. "A more worthless human bein' I never knew."

Roy himself had drifted closer to Jessie's bedside and now reached down to take the girl's hand in his. The gesture was completely opposite in nature to the man's behavior when Connor and Lara had first arrived.

"You've seen a lot of heartbreak, haven't you?" Connor murmured to June.

"No more than most people, but yes, we have."

"Then that makes me even more glad that Lara's here to help your grandchildren." He waited until she turned to look him. "You don't need any more grief than you've suffered already. No one on this earth does."

She gazed at him strangely, but before Connor could decipher her look, his attention was drawn back to Lara, who had finished with her examination of the two girls.

She rose and, hooking her stethoscope

"No!" The older woman raised her head, tears glistening on her cheeks. "It *is* our fault."

She turned on her husband like a Fury. "Roy, I told you we should be takin' the girls to the clinic. I told you. I didn't care if a Brody *was* involved!"

June looked at Connor, who could see that strange expression come to her eyes again— both frightened and mistrusting at once. Frightened and mistrusting not only of him, he realized, but of herself and her own judgment.

Just as Lara had looked at him when he'd leaned in to kiss her.

"Y'see, we knew the Brodys had a hand in the clinic's operation now," June said in a shaking voice. "Then, down at the tack and feed, Roy heard..."

"Heard what?" Connor asked, vaguely aware of how calm his voice sounded. He didn't feel calm, though. Inside, his mind was roaring with the frenzy of a plunging waterfall.

She pressed her lips together briefly, then said, "He heard that no one'd be able to get treatment without payment up front—somethin' about no one getting care 'less they could afford it. We didn't have the money, and Roy here said he'd sooner rot in hell than go beggin' to the son of a murderer."

Connor recoiled as if he'd received a blow to the solar plexus. And in a sense he had. The pain he felt was certainly as cold and sharp and shocking, leaving him breathless.

So. Once more it came down to the fact that he was a Brody. And Brodys weren't to be trusted an inch.

Suddenly Connor felt a weight on his shoulders so heavy it was as if the whole world rested there. Would he be doomed to carry that burden the rest of his natural born days?

THE LOOK RAVAGING Connor's face was that of a man shattered—shattered like a mirror into thousands of shards.

"That's not true!" Lara said. She stepped forward to stand beside Connor in a show of support, facing the McDuffys fearlessly. "No one would be refused treatment, no matter what their circumstances. No one! That's why Connor brought me to Bridgewater and is paying my salary, so the clinic would be staffed with health care professionals who are able to provide treatment whenever it's needed, to anyone."

A thought struck her. "You must have

heard about something I said at the clinic's open house on Halloween—that people would get the best health care affordable." Lara was horrified her words had been turned around to hurt Connor—and now hurt these two little girls. "But I never said people would be turned away if they weren't able to pay! How could you even begin to think such a thing?"

Unfortunately, her hot words brought a defensive spark to Roy McDuffy's eyes. "If you're new to Bridgewater," he said, his chin jutting, "then I guess you wouldn't know the history of what this town—hell, this whole county—has had to put up with from the Brodys. Why, there's a whole laundry list of deeds that—"

"I don't care what Mick Brody did! That's in the past!"

"And that makes what he done any less hurtful or wrong?" Roy argued, sounding enough like Lara herself that she reddened in shame.

"Maybe not, but Connor didn't do anything wrong!" Lara noted how desperate she sounded, as if she were trying to convince herself more than anyone that the past *was* past, and needed to be put to rest once and for all. "How can he be blamed for what his father did?"

"You wanna know how?" Roy retorted. "Because no amount of good deeding can take away the pain and loss of a bad deed! Just 'cause you say you're sorry, that doesn't mean it doesn't hurt like hell when someone stabs you in the back. And even if they patch up the wound with a bandage, that don't necessarily mean it'll heal. The damage is already done!"

He flung an arm out, pointing at the closed door, behind which lay his two very sick granddaughters. "Just like if those two girls of mine suffer some permanent kind of damage from me neglectin' getting 'em medical care, you can be sure I'll be payin' the price alongside of them every day of their lives. I wouldn't blame them if they hated me for it!"

That's when Lara saw the tears of remorse standing in the older man's eyes, before he lowered his chin and dropped his shaking hand slowly to his side.

Yes, Annie and Jessie would heal, but as their grandfather said, some damage was already done.

The silence in the narrow hallway was stultifying. Lara felt drained. Beside her, Connor radiated tension.

Then June spoke, her voice soft. "They

won't blame you, Roy, just as we can't be blamin' Connor here for the sins of his father."

"How can you know that?" Roy asked. "How can you know how Annie and Jessie'll feel years and years from now?"

"Because they'll heal." She took her husband's hand, resisting as he tried to pull away. "They'll heal in the one way that counts—through forgiveness."

Roy said nothing, only turned toward his wife, burying his face in her neck as June McDuffy's arms went round him.

Lara felt Connor's grip on her elbow. She glanced up at him, and he indicated with a tilt of his head that they should leave the McDuffys to themselves. She followed him blindly down the oh-so-familiar stairs and through the house to the back door, surprised when the chilly air hit her face to realize she had tears on her own cheeks. She swiped them away before Connor saw them, although she couldn't have said why.

But she realized the reason once she caught sight of his expression in the gleam of the streetlight. It held a vulnerability she knew well; she saw it in her own eyes as she stared into the mirror each day. And it was obvious Connor had come to the same realization she had.

Yes, real healing came only with forgiveness. But she was as clueless as Connor as to how to find it.

Or how to make it real.

THE RIDE BACK to her house passed in silence. Her mind whirling, her heart aching, Lara clutched the medical bag on her lap, as discouraged as she'd ever been in her life, despite having just done some very good work this evening.

She dared a few glances at Connor, whose face was as immobile as stone, revealing no more of his own thoughts or feelings. When he pulled into her driveway and stopped, making no move to get out, she took his continued silence as a dismissal.

But she couldn't leave it like this!

"Connor..." What could she say, though, to soothe his soul, to soothe both their souls? She had guessed he didn't thank her for jumping to his defense, was angry with her for doing so. Yet she couldn't have prevented herself from speaking up.

"Connor, please," she finally blurted out, not looking at him. "I...it's a long drive to Tanglewood, and you're upset. Won't you come inside for just a few minutes?"

"I'm fine, Lara." His tone was terse. Final.

As final as his father's had been the night he'd shown up on the doorstep and told her mother that Dooley Dearborn had skipped town on account of him.

"No, you're not!" Lara contradicted. "I mean, it's got to be upsetting, getting another hefty dose of the kind of attitude here in Bridgewater that you've been working so hard to change."

"For which I've been criticized, as well."

Lara reddened in shame at his implication, but spoke up firmly. "I'm sorry for saying what I did that afternoon, Connor. It was unfair."

"Apology noted." But not accepted, she noticed. Of course not. The damage had already been done, hadn't it?

Yet he didn't restart the engine, only sat there, his firm jaw working as he stared out the windshield, obviously deep in thought. Deep in turmoil. She watched as he absently rubbed the pad of his thumb along the edge of the leather steering wheel, remembering how it had felt when he had caressed her cheek. As if that merest of touches *could* heal all wounds, no matter how deep.

"You know, it's funny how things work," he finally said, his voice coming from far away, as if he was still lost in his thoughts and trying to find his way back. "I got a call last week from my old boss at the brokerage firm in Fort Worth."

"Really?" It was all she could think to say, although she found herself instantly on guard.

"Yeah. He's opening up an office in Dallas, said he'd love to have me head it up. It'd be close to my mother and stepfather, too. She's been missing me a lot since I moved here." Pensiveness edged his voice as much as the dim light did his profile. "I don't know but that's where I'm meant to be."

Lara's stomach leapfrogged her heart into her throat. Leave? How could he leave?

"You're not seriously considering it, are you?" she challenged. "What about Tanglewood?"

He seemed unconcerned. "Griff's got the ranch well in hand. He could manage it on his own. It wouldn't take more than him checkin' in with me once a week or so by phone to decide on what might need to be done next. And with us partnering with the Bar G on the breeding program, I have no doubt Deke and Addie would be available to give Griff advice or lend him a hand if he needed it."

Connor sounded so matter-of-fact, as if the decision were an easy one. Perhaps it was.

Easier than staying here and enduring more of the town's mistreatment.

Because, after all, what reason had he to stay?

Chapter Seven

She should have known it, seen it coming. She should have—but she hadn't.

Tears gathered at the back of Lara's eyes. Then anger, bubbling hot, boiled up right behind them, its intensity surprising her, even as she let it surface.

She leaned toward Connor, her face coming to within inches of his.

"So you'd go off to Dallas without so much as a by-your-leave, right when some of the projects you've worked so hard on, like the breeding program, are just starting to bear fruit?" she asked. "And wh-what about the clinic?"

He turned on her, eyes blazing. "You'd ask why, after tonight? Lara, you were right—there's no way I'm going to convince people I'm not like my dad, not when the things I do to try to make things better for them are misinterpreted and misjudged time after time. I mean, here I've gone and hired you to bring the kind of community health care to Bridgewater that's so badly needed, and even that's not gonna pass the sniff test with these people!"

The heel of his hand came down with a thump on the edge of the steering wheel, startling her. "What would have happened if I hadn't heard about Annie and Jessie by chance? 'Cause you *know* there were folks who knew about those kids, and weren't going to tell me or you about them!"

The words echoed in the enclosed space. Echoed and then died, as did most of Connor's anger, only to be replaced with that weighty discouragement.

"Most of all," he said quietly, "it's hurtin' you for me to be associated with the clinic. It's keeping you from having the best chance to do the work you came here to do."

He lapsed into a silence wrought with frustration as Lara tried to come up with an argument to refute what he was saying.

Which would be difficult, given that he was right.

"But you simply can't go now," she said stubbornly. "We *are* making headway!"

His brown eyes flared dangerously at her accusing tone. "You call it headway, havin' to practically blindside someone to render medical care, just because I'm a Brody?"

"Well, the Brody I've come to know doesn't run when the going gets tough!" she retorted.

"No, that's pretty much Dearborn territory."

Lara gasped, hurt to her core. She knew he'd meant her—and perhaps justifiably—but the implication she took was that he meant her father.

Connor seemed to come to the same realization a split second later. "Ah, jeez, Lara, I'm sorry," he said, reaching out to her. "I didn't mean it that way—"

But Lara had already turned, found the door handle and vaulted out of the truck, caring not a whit that she confirmed Connor's assertion with her flight.

Reaching her front stoop, she groped frantically in her pocket for her keys, dropping them as she fumbled to find the right one and put it in the lock as the tears threatened to fall again.

"Here, let me," Connor said quietly at her side as he stooped to retrieve the keys.

Shaking, Lara let him, even though she wanted nothing to do with him right now, nothing to do with anyone.

After he opened the door, he lifted his

hand, but the prospect of his mere touch on her shoulder sent her sidestepping away as she passed him to enter the house.

She tossed her medical bag onto the sofa on her way by, heading for her bedroom at the far end of her small bungalow. Heading for that…that minishrine to her long-lost father, for she had to admit that was what it was. A place where she came to find peace through connecting with her father. Or was it to escape facing the reality that, had he really cared, no one, not even Mick Brody, could have made him leave?

In any case, she knew she wouldn't be able to avoid forever the man who *was* here, despite her own suggestion to the contrary.

Behind her, she heard Connor stop at the doorway to her bedroom. "You haven't had the easiest of evenings, either, have you?" he said simply.

He was talking about her reaction to going back to the house where she'd lived. Lara swallowed painfully, hugging herself. She had no desire to go into that ancient history with Connor, especially now. She'd have to give him some answer, though. He wasn't going to leave.

But wasn't that what she most feared?

"It was a shock, to be sure," she said crisply,

very aware of him in her home, in her bedroom. As before, it was as if his presence automatically expanded to fill any space, making her feel vulnerable, as if he'd actually opened the door to her mind and stepped right in. "I guess I knew I'd eventually at least drive past where I used to live. But to find myself standing there at the doorway to the room where—"

She broke off, unable to continue. What was she doing? This was much too dangerous a business, letting him any further into her life, especially when she had even less appreciation than before that he'd be staying.

Yes, it was much too dangerous—being alone with him again.

"Looks like you've added some photos since I was here last," he said, perhaps trying to deflect her obvious distress. The problem was, her thin control over herself became even more stretched by his coming into the room to peer more closely at the collage of framed photos on the wall.

Lara didn't move. She couldn't.

Connor was silent a few moments, apparently absorbing each image. "Your dad and you?" he finally asked, pointing at one, his forearm brushing her shoulder.

"Yes," she said in clipped tones. She took

a deep breath. "Christmas morning. I was only three."

In the photo, she sat on the floor surrounded by bright wrapping paper and boxes, wearing a pair of candy-striped pink footie pajamas with a big grape juice stain down the front. Her white-blond hair was sticking out in every direction and she had a ferocious scowl on her face. Dooley, however, was grinning ear to ear, obviously mightily entertained by his daughter's pique.

Connor chuckled softly, the sound easing the band around her chest ever so slightly. "You don't look in the most Christmasy of moods."

"I believe I had just realized that Santa hadn't brought me the Shetland pony I asked for, and I'd spouted one of Dad's favorite curses."

"What was it?"

"Something to the effect of 'Hell's bells and little antlers, you mean I ain't gettin' a pony?'"

Connor actually chuckled, making the knot in her chest ease even more.

She gazed at the photo with mixed emotions. It was her favorite one of her father, mainly because it was the only picture in which he looked the least bit happy or carefree.

"So. Your father left your mother and you," Connor said quietly.

She'd never heard it expressed in such bald terms. "Yes." Lara swallowed. "So now you know. I haven't got a model father, either."

"Wasn't he? You mean he didn't earn all those medals in Vietnam?"

"Oh, every one of them. But then…he left." She stared at the photo so hard her eyes began to water. "I was four years old."

"I don't get it." Connor pointed to the picture again, his fingertip resting on the lower edge of the oak frame. "Lara, it's obvious he adores you. What could've made him go?"

Lara pivoted, moving away from Connor, her heart pounding out of her chest. Should she tell him? Tell him that it was his father who'd driven home the wedge that had already worked itself into her father's tormented soul and so had propelled him to leave? For she'd heard the arguments between her parents! Dooley, agony in every word, saying it would be better for everyone for him to leave, and Pauline begging him to stay.

Just as she herself had begged Connor to stay only moments before.

"It doesn't matter why Dad left," Lara muttered, shaking her head fiercely. "It's w-water under the bridge. I've got to forgive and forget."

Connor took her by the shoulders and turned her toward him. "But it does matter. Obviously it does, Lara. Because it's coming between us."

Her gaze flew to his and she found his deep brown eyes, even in the meager light from the hallway, as soulful as she'd ever seen them.

"Is there…is there an 'us'?" she whispered.

Frustration bent the edges of his mouth. "I guess that's what I don't have a real handle on. Other than knowin' that there're some things standing in the way of that ever being a possibility. But then—" his gaze dropped "—there are some things on my side, too, standing in our way. Like…how you're right to be kind of mistrustful of me."

Apprehension gripped her. "I am? H-how?"

"When you said I got that Halloween party together to shine up my image in the eyes of—of the townspeople, you weren't entirely wrong." He kept his gaze averted. "But I *do* feel a sense of responsibility to the people of Bridgewater to try and right the wrongs my father committed. And who knows? Maybe that's why I'm failin', because my actions aren't born from a particular concern for people I've come to know individually and as a community over years of livin' and workin' beside them each day. I mean, sometimes I feel like I'm running uphill through three-feet-deep mud. Not only am I makin' no progress, I just keep getting in deeper and deeper because I can't shed the skin that makes me a Brody."

He had a point, Lara thought, her heart filling with compassion for him. He was a Brody, and in these parts it was damning.

Unable to stop herself, she lifted her hand and brushed back a chestnut lock that had fallen across his forehead.

That was when his eyes came back to hers, startling her with their intensity as he gripped her wrist. "But how I am with you, Lara— *who* I am with you—has nothing to do with righting wrongs. All I want is for you to know me for who I am. *Then* decide if there's a chance to be an 'us.'"

His voice grew ragged as he tugged her hand away from his cheek, as if it were too painful for him to endure her touch. "If who I am is someone you don't find yourself likin' or trustin' much, I can handle that. But let those feelings be about *me*—and not about my bein' a Brody."

With that, he turned and headed for the door.

How could she not respond to this man? She wanted so much to tell him that it was within her power to give him the chance he asked for. That she craved it as much as he did. But she wasn't at all certain she could. There was too much history. Too much hurt.

And if she told Connor about the source of that hurt, certainly it would be the last nail in the coffin. And the two of them would never have a chance.

It occurred to her that she wanted that chance, however slim it was, especially now when it seemed it might be snatched away from her. Even scared half to death as she was of what that chance might mean, still she wanted it.

Because all Lara knew for certain was that she couldn't let him go, not if she had it within her power to make him stay.

"I do have feelings that are just about you, Connor," she stated, making him stop short of the doorway.

She cleared her throat, a bid for courage more than time. "I have from the first day I met you when I—I felt such…such a sense of coming home. I don't mean to Bridgewater. I mean within myself."

On trembling legs, she walked over to

stand in front of him. "And the times I've felt it again have been moments like now, when it's just us two... When nothing else matters."

And she lifted her chin to kiss him.

Yet at the first contact of their lips, Connor's head jerked back in shock. His hands came up to grip her upper arms and hold her away from him.

Lara felt her entire body turn hot. Oh, she would die of embarrassment!

"Lara, I gotta admit, I'm confused," he said. "I don't want to take advantage of you. I mean, you've obviously got some issues to work out that aren't going to be settled with good intentions or blockin' out the rest of the world. I won't do that to you, not after what you've been through."

"You're not," she protested. "Taking advantage of me, that is. I'm not four years old any longer, Connor. I'm a big girl."

She tamped down her nervousness and pressed both palms against his chest, lightly kneading the firm flesh beneath the fabric of his shirt. She noticed that he let her, though he didn't relax his grip.

He swallowed, hard. "I don't expect one hundred percent trust up front, you know," he said, tugging her inexorably toward him.

She thought she'd drown in the deep brown depths of his eyes. "I know."

"These things take time...."

"I know."

Then, as if to show her that yes, these things did indeed take time, he didn't kiss her, but cupped his palm under her jaw as he had that first time. Still, his touch was already as moving to Lara as a kiss. Her eyes drifted closed. His breath feathered her cheek, making her knees nearly buckle in anticipation.

Yet he held back, somehow knowing that despite her assurances to the contrary, she was on the edge of flight.

But oh, so much closer to being on the edge of capture.

For then his mouth touched hers, slowly brushing back and forth, sensitizing that flesh in a way that made her feel as if every nerve ending in her body were centered there.

It was exactly as before. This time, however, she wanted more from him. Needed more.

He drew his thumb down the side of her neck to the tender skin there, making her lips part in a sigh. Whether by design or not, she didn't know, but Connor seized upon the advantage to lightly stroke the tender underside of her upper lip with his tongue.

It was still not enough—and more than she could stand. Lara snaked her hands up the hard planes of his chest and muscled neck, past his chiseled jaw to thrust her fingers into his dark hair and finally, finally meld his mouth fully to hers.

Yes, it was more than she had ever imagined, kissing him this way, having him groan in a deep rumble in his chest and kiss her back with such force. He was all male, and focused directly on her right now in that way that was so inherently frightening yet so captivating.

She was hyperaware that they stood in her bedroom, that it was only a few short steps to her bed, where she had yet to give herself to a man. But it had never felt right before this— not as right as this felt with Connor.

Her hands roved over his sandpapery jaw to crescent dimples that she explored first with her fingertips, then, in a move bolder than any she'd ever made in her life, her tongue.

Connor groaned her name, his own hands feverish as he slid them across her rib cage to her waist, to the curve of her hips and up again. With his chin he nudged her head back so that he had access to the sensitive skin of her throat, his own tongue playing havoc with her equilibrium as he kissed her there, making her feel as if she were falling, falling from a cliff a thousand feet high. She was scared and exhilarated at once. Scared that here she stood with the one man she should be most wary of; exhilarated that the connection between them seemed to transcend all other concerns.

That's when she knew: she *was* falling—falling in love with this strong, kind man, despite his name and the blame she must put behind her, once and for all. No, he was not responsible for what his father had done to hers or to anyone else in Bridgewater.

The vow sprang from her heart: Connor must never know the role Mick played in driving her father away and causing such unhappiness in her mother's life, more than her own.

But truly, real and lasting healing would only happen when both of them forgave his father for that.

And when Lara forgave her own father...

She stiffened involuntarily, and Connor immediately broke the kiss. But, thankfully, he didn't let go of her completely this time as he pressed her cheek to his shoulder and held her tightly.

"I'm sorry, Connor—" she began, but he wouldn't let her finish.

"Hush, now. There's nothing to be sorry about." He kissed the top of her head. "It's like I said. These things take time." He took her face in his hands. "That I can deal with, Lara. Because you're right. This Brody doesn't run from things. I'm not goin' to Dallas. I'm here to stay."

She gripped his wrists as he stroked with the pads of his thumbs the tears that had run down her cheeks.

For how could he know those were the four words she most needed from him, and yet were the most difficult to believe in, even now?

"HELLO, DAD."

"Hello, Connor."

Adjusting the microphone closer to his mouth, Connor peered through the bullet-proof glass at his father, across from him in his prison whites.

Father and son sat in the uncomfortable silence that was a staple in these conversations, especially at the beginning.

"Anything goin' on I need to know about since I saw you last?" Mick asked brusquely.

"Not much. Tanglewood is doin' fine,"

Connor volunteered. "I talked to Griff and we decided to put another twenty acres into winter wheat."

"A whole twenty?" Mick looked about to object, but in the end merely shrugged. "I guess that's probably a good idea. Some of those pastures were getting overgrazed."

As usual, there was no "How're you holding up, son?" or any kind of acknowledgment of the responsibility Connor had taken on, nor of the cloud of disgrace he operated under.

"Oh, and the breeding facility over at the Bar G is just about built," Connor added. "Deke Larrabie's been seein' to the finishing touches. We'll start moving Tanglewood stock over there after that."

This he delivered without fanfare, and his father took it the same way. "Fine."

Remembering the package he'd come in with, Connor continued, "I brought you the *Bridgewater Gazette* and some mail that came for you."

Mick nodded in thanks as one of the guards handed him the rubber-band-held bundle, which he set to one side. "It'll give me somethin' to read later."

"That'll be nice," Connor said inanely as the two of them fell into another silence he knew would last for several minutes, now that they had covered the one subject that his father cared about—Tanglewood Ranch.

But such was the nature of Connor's twice-a-month visits to see Mick in Huntsville. It still seemed surreal to him that his own father was living, if one could call it that, in Texas's most famous prison. It was where the hardest cases in the state were locked up.

And, unbelievably, Mick Brody was one of them.

Connor had long struggled with this aspect of his father's guilt. Looking across at him, he was struck, as he always was, by how different Mick appeared. He had diminished, literally, in stature. No longer did he wear the expensive black Stetson that had added a good five inches to his already dominating height, as had the genuine ostrich-skin boots with two-inch stacked heels. Gone as well were the custom-made silver belt buckles that had caught the light and made Connor believe when he was little that his father had somehow lassoed a star and fastened it there at his waist.

Now, though, Mick Brody looked haggard. Beaten. His dark hair was streaked with gray, his normally robust complexion pale and wan.

"You okay, Dad?" Connor asked abruptly. "I mean, you look kind of tired."

Mick shot him one of his old skewering looks. "Oh, I'm just about as dandy as a person can be. Who wouldn't thrive like a weed in this place?"

Connor had to smile. It was the most spirit he'd shown in a long time.

He was surprised when his father sat forward with some energy. "To tell the truth, I've been thinkin'." He snorted. "Not that there's much else to do in this joint." Mick paused, idly worrying the rubber band around the newspaper. "You care to know what I've learned?"

"Of course, Dad."

He tapped his temple with the tip of one index finger. "That the real prison is right here. You can't hide from yourself, you know. The reckoning is always here, and sooner or later you've got to look at yourself in the mirror and see yourself for the man you really are."

Connor was stunned. It was the most self-reflective three sentences he had ever heard come out of Mick Brody's mouth. Maybe, for better or worse, this was the best place for his father right now.

And maybe, for the first time in his life, Connor might have the chance to talk to his father and tell him a little bit about what had made him the man *he* was.

"So what…what do you see there, Dad?"

Mick scowled, tossing the bundle of mail away from him with an abruptness that told Connor this certainly wasn't an easy process for his father. "Too damn much. Oh, there's the good things, like loyalty…and bein' able to love a woman with all your heart."

He stared at a point just past Connor's left shoulder. "And the bad things, like lovin' her too well."

"You mean Deke Larrabie's mother?" Connor dared to ask.

"Of course that's who I mean," Mick said testily. He lapsed into another sullen silence.

Connor waited. Such soul-searching would naturally be difficult for any person; in Mick's case, it was probably like yanking his heart out through his throat.

"I didn't do right by your mama," he finally said, his words barked at Connor through the speaker. "I should've put my feelings for Lorna behind me. But it wasn't something I seemed able to do. Lord, when she came along, I must've been just about the age you are now, maybe a little older, and there I was actin' half as old. Like a blamed fourteen-year-old kid up to my eyeballs in hormones."

Connor had to admit he knew the feeling, much better than he'd have liked to, as he imagined Lara with her every-which-way blond hair, her pink, pouting mouth, and those gray eyes that reminded him of the silver reflection off a still, deep lake.

"I loved her then and love her now, even though she's been dead these twenty-odd years," Mick continued. "I don't know if you'll ever feel that way, son. Part of me hopes you won't, 'cause look where it got me. And you're a Brody, like me."

He gazed at his son steadily, and Connor caught the flicker of something in Mick's eyes that surprised him. Something like real honest-to-goodness fatherly love.

Connor had long ago given up seeing any whisper of that emotion in Mick's eyes. He regularly thanked heaven for having gotten that kind of love from his stepfather, but it had always saddened him that he hadn't experienced such emotion from his own father.

Maybe that was what drew Lara and him together so inescapably, sharing those feelings of loss. Maybe…but Connor didn't think so. They shared feelings, all right, but the connection was much stronger, more elemental. Much more inescapable.

"I think I am," Connor murmured before he thought. "Like you, that is."

Mick's thick eyebrows joined together over his eyes. "You're not still in love with Addie Gentry, are you?"

"No." He shook his head. "No, I realized that a long time ago. It's someone new to town—the physician's assistant I hired for the clinic."

"Oh, yeah. You told me you were lookin' to get someone to take over for Doc Becker. It was a fool's errand then, I'm afraid, and still is. When it comes to people's health, they don't want no outsider tellin' 'em what to do. That means both you and this gal, especially if you're fond of each other."

"Yes, but I've never met anyone like Lara Dearborn."

Through the speaker, Connor heard his father's short intake of breath. It set him on alert.

"That's right, you might know her," he said.

"I can't say as I do," Mick said bluntly.

"Well, maybe not her, but her father," Connor said, watching his father carefully. "Dooley Dearborn worked at Tanglewood about twenty years ago. He'd been a hero in the Vietnam War. Right before he deserted her mother and her."

At this, Mick actually blanched.

"You *do* remember him, don't you, Dad?" Apprehension ate into Connor's stomach like acid. "Do you know what happened to make him leave like that?"

"Why would I?" his father scoffed. "He worked as a hand for a while, no more than eight or nine months." He gestured dismissively. "Hell, Tanglewood's had a thousand of that kind walk through its gate. They come to get enough to make it through the winter, and they quit right after the big money-earning time at roundup."

"Yeah, for those cowboys who don't have families. But Dooley Dearborn had a wife and little girl—"

"Looks like my time's up." Mick turned abruptly, as if his name had been called. Connor noticed the guard to one side hadn't moved a muscle.

What was going on here? Something involving Lara's father.

"Dad, wait—" he protested, but Mick had already hung up the receiver.

Connor could only sit dumbly as he watched his father walk, without a backward glance, toward the guard, who unlocked the door to the prison cell that Mick obviously preferred to telling his son the truth.

What had happened all those years ago between his father and Lara's? What wasn't Mick telling him?

Another thought struck him, turning his guts to water. What if Lara *did* have a legitimate, very personal reason to mistrust the Brodys, mistrust him?

All Connor knew was, if that was true, he didn't want to know about it.

LISTENING TO HER mother and Aunt Frannie good-naturedly carp at each other as they bustled around the Corbin kitchen, Lara wondered what she had been so worried about.

Pauline had surprised her earlier in the week by announcing she was ready to visit her in Bridgewater—then had shown up on Lara's doorstep two days later. Of course, it was what Lara had hoped would happen ever since she'd moved back to town. She had always thought that it would benefit Pauline to come back to this place where so many unresolved hurts lingered, and lay them to rest.

However, that was before Lara had discovered how many of her own ghosts still haunted her. Before she had begun to fall in love with Connor Brody.

"Don't you dare use margarine in that cake frosting," Pauline warned her sister-in-law as Frannie unwrapped a stick of Olco, preparing to drop it into the mound of powdered sugar in a mixing bowl.

"I never used to, believe me. Then I turned fifty and started listening to all those warnings about fat on the evenin' news," Frannie said somewhat wistfully.

Pauline snatched the bowl away. "I know we're both of an age where we need to be mindful of what we eat, but not when there's a celebration goin' on." She plopped into the sugar the stick of real butter that had been softening on the counter, added the package of cream cheese that had been doing the same, and handed the bowl back to Frannie. "Now, it's time to splurge, just for a little while."

"Celebration? What celebration?" Griff asked, sauntering into the kitchen as his mother glared good-naturedly at her sister-in-law.

"Oh, bein' together again with cherished family members, what else?" she sniffed, making everyone laugh.

Leaning her elbows on the kitchen table,

Lara sighed in contentment. It had been over a year since the two families had been together. The Corbins always came to Dallas to visit, since it was easier for other relatives from out of state to travel there and meet for family gatherings. Easier on Pauline, too, than returning to Bridgewater.

But now there were two missing: Web Corbin and Dooley Dearborn. That fact brought them together, despite the memories here.

Lara could almost forget what those memories were, too. Almost.

Absently, she folded the dish towel that lay crumpled on the counter in front of her. She hadn't told her mother about Connor yet. Of course, what was there to tell? The feelings between them were still so new and fresh— and fragile. At least on her part.

She knew, though, that if she'd told her mother nothing at this point, it had less to do with the newness of feelings between herself and Connor than with the fact that he was a Brody.

"So if we're celebrating, does that mean the more the merrier?" Griff asked, slipping around his mother's back to swipe a fingerful of frosting. He deftly dodged her slapping spatula.

"Why, sure," Frannie said. "There's plenty to eat. Who'd you have in mind?"

At the slam of a car door, the innocent light that came to her cousin's eyes caused Lara's contentment to vanish, and immediately put on her guard. "I do believe that's him now," Griff said.

There was a knock at the back door, and in walked Connor.

Chapter Eight

Supper at the Corbins' was as tense an affair as Connor had endured in a long time, his visits with his father notwithstanding.

First of all, it was a surprise to find Lara's mother, Pauline, was in town. Lara hadn't said a word about her visit. Not that he and Lara relayed every detail of their lives to each other. But in the few weeks since they'd shared those intimate moments in her darkened bedroom, they'd fallen into a habit of touching base with each other every few days. To talk, if nothing else. To touch, if there was any way he could manage it.

He was trying to give her room, to take it slowly, as he'd promised. He sensed with Lara he was still on tenuous ground, where any moment she might withdraw. And run.

And never had she seemed more poised to flee than this evening. When he'd walked through the door, the look on her face could only have been described as pure panic. He took his cue and introduced himself to her mother as a friend of Griff's only, although Griff apparently had no scruples about volunteering that Connor was also his boss—and Lara's.

He'd have had to have been blind, however, not to catch the look of shock that sprang to Pauline Dearborn's gentle gray eyes, so like her daughter's, at hearing the Brody name, making the conversation he'd had last week with his father echo warningly in his head. And making the discouragement he always experienced at such moments multiply tenfold. Yet for Lara's sake, he'd managed to act as if it didn't affect him a whit.

Keeping up the charade was wearing on him, though, as Connor listened to Mrs. Corbin go on about the trial it had been to stitch a quilt for an upcoming raffle. Something about running out of a certain color of green thread and having to drive all the way into Houston twice to find a match.

He was brought out of his musings by Mrs. Dearborn's soft voice. "I'd love to take a drive around town after supper and see some of the old places I used to know," she said, her eyes shining with nostalgia. "Does Hawk Jacobs still run that old-fashioned Dairy Corner?"

"Sure does, Aunt Pauline," Griff volunteered around a mouthful of mashed potatoes.

Her eyes turned incandescent at his words, and Connor knew then where Lara had gotten both her gray eyes and her idealistic bent. "Remember how we'd walk down on a summer's evening and get an ice cream, Lara?"

"Y-yes," Lara virtually mumbled, her gaze fastened on her uneaten food.

Pauline didn't seem to notice. "And I'd love to go by the old house. I wonder if whoever lives there would let us in for a look around?"

There was a short pause, then Lara said quietly, "The McDuffys live there. I... A few weeks ago I went there to treat their two granddaughters for strep throat." She threw a quick, almost guilty glance his way. "Connor had learned they were sick one evening when he was at the Diamond Tap."

He waited for her to add how he'd driven her to the McDuffys, had run interference around Roy McDuffy to get her in the door. Had let her lean on him as she'd let him lean on her afterward, in a way that had filled his soul as much as it had his heart.

"So. Connor." Pauline cleared her throat, as if by way of gathering courage. "I hear you're at Tanglewood for now?"

"Not just for now," he answered definitely. "For good."

The two older women exchanged looks that told him he'd been the topic of at least one conversation between them since Lara's mother had arrived in town.

"But I'd understood your father would be... was supposed to have..." Frannie's voice trailed off awkwardly.

"That he'd be out of prison in four years and back in charge of Tanglewood?" Connor answered baldly. He'd learned that was the best way. "People seem to forget that I'd come back to the ranch to learn the ropes so that I could take over for Dad *before* he was convicted of killing D. K. Larrabie."

He noted each woman's sharp intake of breath at his bluntness, realizing only then how that bluntness had been as much a part of his father's personality as Mick's signature was. And was apparently as indelibly etched into their minds.

"Speaking of Tanglewood, I hope you'll excuse me, but I need to get back." There was nothing to be gained by continuing to become acquainted with Lara's mother, he could tell. It would have been nice to put his best foot forward and make a good first impression, but that seemed impossible when his name preceded him wherever he went. And who knew what particularly scarring imprint his father had left on Lara's family?

Maybe that was what Lara had tried to prevent by keeping her mother's visit from him. Somehow, he couldn't find it in him to thank her for it.

His chair scraped loudly on the wood floor as he pushed it away from the table. "Thank you for the fine meal, Mrs. Corbin."

Frannie looked up in startled dismay. "Won't you stay, Connor? Pauline made a wonderful carrot cake, and I—"

He didn't hear the rest, since he was already halfway to the door. Grabbing his hat from the peg on the wall, he crammed it on his head as he descended the back steps in one stride.

His thoughts were agitating like a washing machine, so much that he didn't hear Lara calling after him till he'd reached his pickup. "Connor, wait! Please!"

He stopped, fingers on the door handle, but couldn't make himself turn around.

"I'm sorry for how I acted tonight," she said from behind him. "Not being more... open with my family about our relationship."

"Yeah, it was pretty obvious the last thing you wanted was for your mother to suspect you'd have any truck with a Brody, let alone special feelings." He couldn't stop himself from saying it.

"It wasn't that!" she denied hotly.

He spun around, hitting her with his gaze. "It wasn't?"

At least she had the good grace to blush. "Not exactly. Oh, it's hard to explain!"

He shifted his weight onto one leg, arms crossed. "I'm all ears."

She ran her palms nervously down the front of her khaki slacks. "There are things I can't tell you. What I *can* tell you is that I'm trying my best to resolve those issues." She gazed at him with those luminous eyes that made him feel as if he didn't have a bone in his body. "For us."

"Well, it'd help if you'd give me even a hint of what you're talking about," he said stubbornly. Because yes, he did want to know what it was his father had avoided telling him, even though the prospect made his dinner lurch dangerously in his stomach. The truth had to be better than not knowing.

Yet it wasn't to be.

"I can't," Lara said. "I can't talk to you about it yet. And you're just going to have to give me some breathing room until I can."

Her gray eyes turned pleading. "For once, you're going to have to trust *me,* Connor."

Torn, he gazed down at her beautiful, earnest face and felt himself weaken. Let himself weaken. He hesitated, then gave a short nod. "All right."

She rose on tiptoe to give him a brief peck on the cheek, but when he turned his head, wanting more, needing more, and their lips touched, he was gratified that she was as helpless as he to stop there. Within moments, the kiss had deepened; the caresses had grown passionate as he crushed her to him, wanting never to let her go.

God, he loved her. How he had fallen so hard and so fast, he couldn't have said. All he knew was that he couldn't deny her anything, that he would have promised her the moon right then if she'd asked for it.

Was this how his father had felt about Deke Larrabie's mother—consumed, all of himself caught up in all of her, so that to take a breath without her seemed like not living at all?

The two women even had similar names: Lorna and Lara.

He lifted his head, his gaze roving over Lara's upturned face, her eyes still closed as if in a trance, her lips glistening from the kiss that had put her in such a state. Lord, he wanted nothing more than to continue to kiss her, to carry them both away on a tidal wave of sensation and emotion. But he couldn't do that. He wouldn't do that to her.

Connor cleared his throat. "I'll let you get back to your family," he said, releasing her abruptly and climbing into his truck. He drove away without a backward glance, not trusting himself to look at her again.

Instead, Connor stared out the windshield, his jaw clenched so hard it throbbed. Sure, he had promised her patience and understanding. But he was finding himself to be more of a Brody than he'd ever have believed he could be.

THE REST OF the evening passed in a haze for Lara. After Connor left, the four of them finished eating, and decided to postpone the ride around town when it started to sprinkle outside.

Rain was falling in earnest by the time Lara and her mother pulled into her garage. Though they made a dash for the back door, they ended up getting a soaking.

Lara didn't mind. It was like a balm on her soul to set the teakettle boiling after she and her mother had changed into dry clothes. Raindrops pattered against the windows, blown by the wind, making it just that much more cozy inside her little house.

"Earl Grey, right?" she said as she set a full mug trailing a tea bag string on the table in front of her mother before sitting kitty-corner to Pauline with her own mug of piping-hot herbal tea.

"Right." Pauline clasped the mug in both hands, letting the steam warm her face. She smiled as Lara did the same. "Just like old times, isn't it?"

Lara blew on the pale brown liquid, causing ripples. "Yes."

While the setting was different, the ritual was as familiar as an old shoe to Lara, comforting her and soothing her jangled nerves.

"I'm glad you came to visit, Mom," she said. "Even though I know it's hard for you. You know, being back in Bridgewater again, after so long."

"Mmm." Her mother concentrated on cooling down her own tea, her forehead puckered. "I'll admit it was a shock seein' Mick Brody's son in Frannie's house. I can see how it must have thrown you to come down here to start working in the clinic and find out a Brody was paying your salary."

Lara managed not to react visibly. She had hoped to explore this subject with Pauline while she was here. Hoped, as she'd promised Connor, to resolve and lay to rest the issues she knew she must if the two of them were to have a chance.

"It was probably more of a shock to you than me," Lara said matter-of-factly. "I never met Mick Brody—only heard him when he came to our home that evening."

Pauline reached up to brush a lock of Lara's hair out of her eyes with that protectiveness mothers never lose for their children. "No child should have had to hear that kind of thing about her daddy. I must say, though, Connor seems nice. And Griff said he's the best boss and friend a person could have, that he's no ordinary man."

That, Lara could agree with, remembering how it had felt to be engulfed in those strong arms of his, so that she'd never wanted to know life without them around her. Yet there had been a note of doubt in her mother's approving words.

"I sure don't have any complaints as to how Connor's dealt with me as an employee," Lara stated loyally, though she continued to stare into the amber depths of her mug of tea.

"I didn't think you did."

She felt her mother's gaze upon her. "I

guess I mean I don't want you to worry about me…about me and Connor Brody, Mom."

"Worry—how?"

"That he'll take advantage of me—that is, he won't cheat me or lie to me. He *is* what Griff said," she averred. "He's no ordinary man."

But her words sounded too emphatic even to her own ears.

As if she'd heard it, too, Pauline said softly, "He's just a man, though."

Lara's head came up. "What do you mean?"

"Only that…no one's perfect, honey."

Her mother spoke as if to a child. "I think I've figured that out already, Mom," Lara said drily. "About a *lot* of people."

"Even…yourself?"

She peered at her mother in curiosity. "What are you getting at, Mom?"

Pauline sighed. "Oh, I don't know. Only that…I think it *is* very hard to come to terms with our own faults and foibles, even when we're older. We have to live with ourselves every day, though. And at some point you either face your own nature and accept yourself for who you are, or you go on staring past the problem."

She ran the tip of her finger ruminatively around the rim of her mug. "I think that's why it's sometimes harder to come to terms with the flaws...even the frailties...of those we love. We're not inside their heads and hearts, so we can't see what they would rather die than have us know about them."

Pauline gazed at Lara lovingly—in that way parents never lose of wanting so greatly to protect their children from the world, while knowing that no one can. "And when they do—hide themselves from us, that is—it keeps us from accepting them, and loving them, with all our heart. And without that, no one will ever find real, complete happiness. You know?"

Lara stared at her mother. It sounded as if Pauline was warning her about something. Or someone.

Was it Connor? Was Lara being naive, letting him into her heart? For the doubts she had about any future they might have together were very real. Was it because no matter what kind of man he showed himself to be, deep down he was still a Brody? And while that doubt seemed to disappear when she was in his arms, was that going to be enough? she wondered. Was she kidding herself to even begin to try?

She looked up to find her mother's gaze upon her, as loving and understanding as ever, yet with a new emotion showing there, way at the back, that Lara had never seen before.

Was Pauline warning her...about someone else?

Lara glanced at the clock on the stove. "Gosh, is it that late? I have appointments starting at 7:00 a.m. tomorrow."

She rose, wrapping her robe more tightly about her, telegraphing her intent to leave.

She could guess the reason behind Pauline's next sigh. "Then you'd better get to bed. I think I'll sit here for a while, if that's all right."

"Of course."

"Good night, dear."

"'Night, Mom," Lara said as she headed for her bedroom, her feeling of comfort completely gone. She could have asked her mother what she'd meant. Yet she hadn't.

No, she hadn't. And was it truly because she didn't want to know—or was it that she knew already, and the last thing in the world she wanted was for her mother to guess that she did?

CONNOR PUSHED OPEN the clinic's front door with barely a whisper of effort.

He smiled to himself. *Good.* He'd taken

the door down himself last week and planed it, then weather-stripped the bottom. No longer would it take Jesse Ventura to wrestle it open. Anyone from the smallest child to an octogenarian bent with arthritis would have no trouble accessing the clinic.

Of course, it also meant he had one less reason to stop by to see if he could help Lara out in any way.

He knew he shouldn't have come at all today, but he'd just wanted a glimpse of her, to say hello and to hear her soft voice as she said hello back.

Damn, but he had it bad.

Connor wandered toward the back of the clinic to find one exam room empty and the door to the other shut. Lara must be in there with a patient. He knew from experience that Bev was often needed to assist, depending who was being treated and for what.

Then he heard feminine voices coming from the small break room at the end of the hallway. Thinking it was Lara and Bev, he'd started toward them when he realized who in fact was talking.

Connor stopped dead in his tracks. It was Frannie Corbin and Pauline Dearborn.

"So each patient's file gets color-coded labels for the first three letters of their name, plus a file label with their name typed on it. Is that how it works?" Connor heard Pauline ask.

"Yes," Frannie answered. "It's a new system for tracking patients that Connor set up. Something about being able to cross-reference people from a database to their physical record so anyone can locate it in seconds. It'll make things a whole lot easier, Lara said, for her and Bev, and a whole lot safer for people comin' here."

Connor couldn't help his chest swelling a bit at the thirdhand praise. So it seemed the two women were doing some clerical work for Lara. He was debating whether to greet them or walk silently back to the front of the building to wait for her when he heard his name again.

"You know, Pauline, Connor Brody's done some mighty fine things in this town since comin' here, and not just at the clinic," Frannie said. "He's been a godsend to Griff—and me. After Web died, Connor gave Griff as much time off as he needed, even though he'd just started working at Tanglewood, to settle back in here in Bridgewater. He gave Griff a raise soon after that, too, sensing he needed the extra income—for me."

This time guilt ballooned in him. He

shouldn't be listening to the ladies' private conversation. Still, he didn't move a muscle.

"I've got to believe you're singin' Connor's praises for only one reason, Frannie," Pauline stated. "And that's because Lara's fallen in love with him."

Leaning back against the wall, Connor closed his eyes. He wasn't sorry in the least to have heard that.

"She told you that?" Frannie asked with evident surprise.

"Not in so many words, no. But anyone lookin' at her when he's around or when his name is mentioned could figure it out."

Was it just him, or did he detect apprehension in her voice?

"Lara could do worse," Frannie said reassuringly, as if in answer to his silent question. "He's a fine young man, even if he is Mick Brody's son."

"Yes, Mick Brody..." Connor heard Lara's mother sigh. "I'm afraid it was more of a shock than I thought it would be, seeing his son the other night. Not that I could ever blame the young man. I don't know that I could still blame Mick."

Connor's eyes flew open. *What?*

There was another sigh from Pauline, this one much more rife with distress. "It's been a long time since I've thought about what happened here in Bridgewater. A long, long time."

"Have you forgiven him, then?" Frannie asked softly.

What had happened here in Bridgewater that Pauline Dearborn might need to forgive Mick Brody for? Connor recalled both Lara's and her mother's immediate reaction of fear upon meeting him for the first time. He'd thought it was simply the Brody reputation preceding him.

But then there was Mick's evasion about Lara's father....

Something told Connor that he was about to find out what it was that it seemed no one—not his father, nor Lara and now her mother—wanted him to know.

The scrape of a chair across the floor told him that Lara's mother was as troubled as he.

Foreboding nipped at his insides even as Connor pressed himself even closer to the wall. He couldn't risk being found out now. He *had* to know!

"Oh, Frannie, I don't know!" Her voice, wrought with anguish, was much closer. Connor realized she stood just on the other side of the wall from him, which ratcheted his dread up a good dozen notches. "I suppose

I thought I had forgiven him. Or at least felt I'd put what happened behind me, for Lara's sake if no other."

"You *had* to move on," Frannie murmured. "You had a daughter to raise, and you made a fine job of it, even with that big uncertainty always in the background, like a storm cloud on the horizon."

What uncertainty? Connor thought in a near fever.

"Yes. Yes, I've got to remember that. Lara's turned out to be a fine young woman with a wonderful life ahead of her. All I want is for her to be happy."

"And what about your happiness?" Griff's mother gently reminded Pauline. "You've never remarried, you know."

"No, I didn't." Her voice trembled. "How could I, though, when I still loved him so?"

Connor shook his head in confusion. Who was she talking about having forgiven: his father—or Lara's? What had happened all those years ago, that he'd been able to see the shock waves still echoing in both Lara's and Pauline's eyes?

He dropped his chin, listening hard, afraid he would never find out. But then Pauline finally went on in a whisper, "I loved Dooley then, despite everything, and I still love him, even though I know I shouldn't. Because he's never coming back."

She paused, the painful catch in her breath, the cracking of her voice, even of her heart, as audible to him as if panes of glass had shattered all around him.

Some impulse caused him to raise his head. At the entrance to the hallway stood Lara, her gray eyes huge in her face as she and Connor listened to her mother go on.

"It was like my world had come to an end when Mick Brody showed up at my door that night and told me he'd fired Dooley and run him out of town."

A world of hurt radiated in those words. A world of dashed hopes that could never be resurrected from the millions of fragments, making Connor's own heart die within his chest.

"I knew then it was over," Pauline whispered, "and I'd never see my husband again."

LARA PRESSED HER fingers to her mouth to stifle her gasp of pain, for it was as if she felt the blow that struck Connor with her mother's admission.

He knows. He knew now what awful role Mick Brody played in her life.

Oh, she'd give anything for him not to have

found out! She'd wanted to tell him herself, in her own way and her own time.

But she'd waited, wanting to settle things in her heart first. Wanting to work toward forgiveness of the father so that she could love the son freely.

"Oh, Connor—" she whispered.

Not looking at her, he started past her. She couldn't let him go like this. Her hand shot out to grasp his forearm, and it was as if she held on to a live wire, the tension under her palm was so palpable. Her move forestalled his leaving for only a moment as he stared at her hand on his arm. Then, without a word, he carefully removed it and continued past her to the door. It opened and closed as smoothly as silk.

Of course. Because he'd fixed it just last week.

"Lara?"

She turned, trying to blink back the tears that filled her eyes. Her mother and aunt stood at the doorway of the break room, puzzled concern creasing their brows.

"Lara, what's wrong?" Her mother came forward, glancing around.

So they hadn't seen Connor. Somehow she felt she needed to protect him right now, though she couldn't have said why.

"Nothing's wrong," she lied.

"But you're crying!" Pauline took her elbow. "What is it, dear?"

"Actually, I—I just got off the phone with a mother whose three-year-old had choked on a piece of apple." She scraped her fingers across her wet cheeks. "She was able to clear the blockage with the maneuver I'd shown her in a CPR class." Lara managed a watery smile. "It was pretty emotional, but in a good way, you know?"

"Why, that's wonderful!" Frannie said, coming from behind Pauline and giving Lara a hug. "Heavens, do you realize what might have happened to that child if you had never come to Bridgewater to practice?"

Lara hugged her aunt back, then released her and turned away before either of the other women saw what she wanted to hide more than the tears.

And that was the shameful wish that she had done exactly that: never come to Bridgewater.

Not for her own sake, however. For Connor's.

Chapter Nine

Tanglewood.

The word, written in white wrought iron that glowed in the evening light, spanned the arch over the entrance to the ranch.

From behind the wheel of her car, Lara could only sit and stare out the windshield at the sign. She had never been here before. Never set foot on Brody property. Never wanted to. It represented so much that was insurmountable to her. The sheer breadth of land it covered that seemed to go on without boundary, until what the Brodys didn't own seemed trifling compared to what they did. The number of cattle rumored to roam its hills and valleys seemed limitless.

The power that land and its bounty brought with it were the most incalculable of all.

She couldn't help but give a shiver as she drove beneath the lintel sign and up the long, majestic drive to the main house, where she hoped against hope to find Connor.

Only for him would she have dared make this trip.

The long, low ranch house at first appeared completely dark as her car tires crunched to a stop on the gravel, making her heart sink.

But no—there was a light on toward the back of the house. It looked pretty lonely, though, all by itself.

Getting out of the car, she felt her throat tighten in empathy.

She took a deep breath, knocked on the wide oak front door. And waited.

After knocking three times, Lara decided either no one was home or someone was choosing not to answer her knock.

Well, she wasn't going to be so easily discouraged.

She picked her way around the side of the house by the scant illumination afforded by the intermittent landscape lights that lit the pale gold brick facade of the home. It certainly was a magnificent house. She couldn't see much of the scenery beyond the white pipe fencing surrounding the ranch house, but she'd bet it was pretty stunning, as well.

What would it be like to live here? she wondered. *Probably like living in a castle surrounded by a moat, for all one might feel connected to the real world.*

After stubbing her toe twice in the dark, Lara finally found the back entrance, where she set to pounding on the door, with the same results.

She hugged herself against the mid-November chill. Where in Billy blue blazes *was* he? she wondered, stepping back from under the awning to see if there were any signs of life inside the house. He wouldn't have left town, would he? He'd promised her he'd stay!

Panic lit within her and fanned to flame. He couldn't go!

"Dad-blame it, Connor Brody, where have you taken yourself off to?" she shouted at the house in sheer frustration.

"I'm right here."

Lara jumped, letting out a small screech of surprise. She whirled, peering into the gloom. "Connor?"

He was leaning back in a lounge chair on the brick patio, his booted feet crossed at the ankles and his hat tipped forward on his brow, with his hands linked behind his neck. He looked for all the world as if he hadn't a care in his head, and she'd worried about him for nothing.

"How could you!" Lara demanded.

"How could I what?" he echoed blandly.

"How could you let me knock if you were right here all the time?" she asked hotly.

She saw his shoulders move in a shrug. "I guess I was wondering just how determined you'd be—whether you'd brave stepping onto the power-hungry landowner's property in order to find me or run along back home where you'd be safe and sound."

He set his boots on the ground and pushed himself upright, coming toward her with a slow, stalking step. "Especially when you weren't so sure I wasn't as dangerous as some spaghetti Western cattle king—or actually, the just-as-wicked son?"

She gulped, not backing up an inch. "You're not like your father, Connor. I know that now."

"Aren't I?" The shadows played across his features, making the dimples on either side of his sternly set mouth appeared cavernous. "I wouldn't be so sure of that, Lara. What's the saying? Blood will out. You can't escape who you are. Or what you are."

"And you're *not* like your father!" she retorted.

He took another step toward her. "Care to test that claim? 'Cause I'm guessing I'm this close to being able to run off another Dearborn, if I choose to."

She'd never seen him like this. Never heard him so implacable—except once, when he'd told her she was on her own. And yes, it did frighten her. Clearly, he was devastated by this latest evidence of his father's destructive machinations in people's lives, more like the king of Olympus than king of the West.

"Connor. I'm not *my* father, either," she said, her voice shaking only the tiniest bit. "I'm not leaving. Not until we've talked this out. You owe me that much."

He stared down at her, and for a fleeting moment she thought he'd make good on *his* claim. Then he pivoted, taking half a dozen steps away from her. His movements somehow triggered a motion sensor, which promptly illuminated them and the patio in the beam of a floodlight.

It seemed eerily symbolic of the scene playing out between them to shed light—unwelcome, glaring—on secret fears both of them had long hidden inside.

"You shouldn't have come, Lara," Connor finally growled.

"I had to. I need to explain about what you heard today—"

"Don't you see, Lara?" He spun to face her

again. "There're some things that are beyond explainin'. They just *are*."

He jabbed a finger at the ground in emphasis. "Like how I'm the son of Mick Brody, the man who's responsible for your dad's leaving—"

He broke off, his Adam's apple working in his throat. Her own throat ached with unshed tears of empathy for him as he found the ability to add, through clenched teeth, "Like how it'll never change the hurt you've held inside you your whole life because of that."

His eyes met hers then, and Lara gasped, for what she saw in his deep brown eyes was how he ached for *her* loss…and the loss of what might have been between them.

He obviously glimpsed that understanding in her eyes, for he said raggedly, "It's hopeless, isn't it, Lara? You're never gonna be able to completely trust me—not like a woman needs to trust the man she'll spend the rest of her life with."

She pressed her palm to her lips to stifle her sob of despair. Certainly, if he didn't believe they had a chance, how was she to?

He shook his head sadly. "Shoot, Lara, I can see it in your eyes right now how you have doubts about me."

He was right. All of her old mistrust rose

up around her in a miasma. But was he also right that she'd never be able to look into his eyes and have both of them know in their hearts that the trust they had was complete?

"These things—trust, I mean—take time," she reminded him. "You've said so yourself, again and again."

"Yes, but that was before I knew what had happened. That's what you were flashing back to at the McDuffys', wasn't it? How you were there when my dad came to your house and told your mother Dooley was gone, on account of him."

"Yes!" she cried, wanting to clap her hands over her ears, then over her eyes, to block out what he was saying, it sounded so much as if he were giving up. So much like her father had sounded those years ago. "But why does that mean there's no chance between us?"

"You got any idea how to change the past?" he asked. "If you do, then I'm sure as hell listenin'. 'Cause that's what it'd take, I'm afraid."

"We could try, couldn't we?" she asked desperately. "What would it hurt to try?"

"A lot, I'm thinking. I'm afraid it would cause you much more damage than good if we got in any deeper with each other and it *didn't* turn out. I won't be the man to do that to you, Lara. Not again."

Lara had no reply for him. What he said was true, at least as much as she knew the truth to be at this moment. And there seemed little chance that anything could change. Not her father's actions, not Mick's.

And consequently, not the two children of those men.

No, she had no clue how to change anything, including the love she felt for him, which was tearing her apart.

Lara sniffed back a sob, but it found its way past her lips, along with another, then another. And she suddenly found herself wrapped within Connor's strong, warm embrace. Knowing that it might be the last time she experienced that comfort made her cry all the harder. She threw her arms about his neck, making him hug her that much tighter.

"Lara. Don't cry, darlin'. It'll be all right," he soothed, but it was clear from the hoarseness of his voice that he had no belief that things *would* be fine. Nothing would be the same for either of them after this.

Still, she couldn't let him go!

Lifting her head, she met his gaze. She didn't begin to pretend to hide what was in her heart.

"Lara." The word was a warning. "It wouldn't be right. You know that. You'd be best to leave. Right now."

But he didn't let her go.

Still, his features had drawn tight as he tried to maintain control over himself. Well, she wouldn't have it. She would make this as difficult on him as it was on her.

Lara drew in a shaky breath, pressing her breasts against his chest, and she could tell that simple contact was wreaking havoc on him. She didn't care. She curled her fingers into the hair at the nape of his neck, like a cat flexing its claws, as she pressed into the cradle of his hips.

They both gasped.

"Lara," he growled.

"Kiss me, Connor," she begged shamelessly. "Just once before I go. You owe me that much."

The light had thrown his face half into shadow, and she couldn't make out the expression in his eyes. But his jaw was set like stone.

She wondered for a brief, frightening moment if he would gain control over himself and push her away.

Then—oh, heaven!—with a guttural groan he crushed her against him, taking her mouth in what could never have been called a kiss. It was much too consuming, much too primitive, with the bruising of tender flesh against teeth, the probing of intimate recesses with tongues that quested thirstily and wouldn't be denied.

Lara felt herself being caught up in a haze of sheer emotion as Connor lifted her closer still, and she wrapped her legs around his waist in a move that was as daring as anything she'd ever done in her life, drawing a rasped oath from him.

He was worth it, though. He was worth the risk of coming out of her comfort zone. Of trusting when she had none of the answers, nor even knew the questions she should be asking.

Because this *was* much too primitive, too fundamental. Much too complete a melding of not just lips and bodies, but minds, hearts and souls.

She knew it, because in the next moment Connor broke the kiss. His hands on her waist lifted her away from him to set her back on the ground. And it was like breaking a law of nature.

Still, they stood locked in each other's arms for several moments, their foreheads touching, breathing ragged, hearts pounding.

Finally, Lara lifted her head with fierce purpose. "You can't make me believe it," she said. "There's no way with this...*this* between us that we can't be together."

"Being together, though, doesn't mean everyone lives happily ever after, Lara." Hadn't her mother said something to that effect? "We both saw that with our parents. The past is what it is. We're who we are."

He drew one fingertip down the side of her cheek, his gaze following its path. "It's better, I think, not to let ourselves go much deeper with each other. Every time we do, it just brings us more pain. And I can't stand that. Not for myself, but for you."

"And m-me for you," Lara choked out, although she couldn't imagine feeling much more pain than was piercing her entire being right now. "You've got to believe that, Connor."

"I do." He let her go then, pushing away from her almost violently. Head down, he commanded, "Go!"

Tears blinding her, Lara stumbled across the patio. She turned at its edge. Connor stood looking after her, his fingers crammed into the front pockets of his jeans as if he didn't trust himself not to reach out for her again.

Of going after what he wanted, and the rest of the world be damned.

"Would you like me to resign from the clinic, leave Bridgewater altogether?" she asked. "I will, if it'll make it easier for you."

He sighed heavily. "Of course I don't want you to. But you have to do what's best for you, Lara."

The automatic light clicked off at that moment, plunging them into relative darkness. All she could see was his tall, lean silhouette.

"I know I'd leave Bridgewater, if I believed it'd do any good," he stated. "But it's become pretty clear to me that the world out there isn't big enough for me ever to escape who I am."

LARA DISCOVERED SHE was the kind of person who could lose herself in her work. Almost.

"All right, then, Kelly," she said, placing an adhesive bandage over the site where she'd just administered a tetanus shot. "No more climbing through old barbed-wire fences while playing hide-and-seek, okay?" she told the youngster perched on the edge of the examining table, cowboy-booted feet dangling.

A jagged rip in one jeans leg revealed another bandage patched over the nasty scrape that was the reason for this visit to Lara's clinic in the first place.

"Yes, Miss Dearborn," said the dark-haired little girl in question. She was a real pistol, Lara could tell, despite the angelic look in her long-lashed green eyes.

Her second-grade teacher, standing behind her with her arms crossed, confirmed the assessment. "She's going to have some time to think about it, at any rate," Julia Sennett said. "You and I are going to be spending the next week's recesses together," she said to the little girl.

"Aw, shoot! Really?" Kelly exclaimed with a scowl. Somehow Lara wasn't convinced of the little child's pique. Quite obviously, teacher and student were fond of each other.

"Hop down," she instructed her patient. "You can go on out and see if Nurse Bev has a sucker for you. Unless you're too old for them."

"Oh, sure I am," the girl said blithely, "but I take all the candy I can get."

Chuckling, Lara and the teacher followed Kelly out of the examining room to the foyer, where Lara signed the treatment form and handed it to Julia.

Something apparently clicked in her brain at seeing Lara's name in print. "That's right!" she exclaimed. "You're Griff Corbin's cousin, aren't you? He's told me so much about you."

Lara's eyebrows rose. "He has?"

"All good, I assure you." She laughed. "Griff and I are old friends. We've known each other since we were born, literally."

The way she said it, with such affection, made Lara peer at her in curiosity. She certainly wasn't Griff's type—tall, with long, honey-gold hair and intelligent hazel eyes. On the whole, he liked his women dark-eyed and petite.

Then Lara spied the engagement ring on her left ring finger.

"Oh, you're getting married?" she asked.

Julia gracefully extended her arm. "Yes, to a man I've also known since childhood." She gave another laugh, this one wry. "We're awfully insular here in Bridgewater, in case you haven't figured it out. We all know the worst and best about each other, usually for at least a couple of generations back."

And apparently never forget or forgive, Lara thought, but didn't say it. Wasn't she herself the poster child for that sentiment?

She saw Julia and her pupil out, and was helping Bev close up for the evening when the phone rang.

"I'll get it, Bev," she told the nurse. "You go on home."

Watching the older woman close the door

behind her, Lara picked up the receiver. "Bridgewater Clinic."

"Oh, Lara, good. I was hoping you'd be there," said the masculine voice on the other end.

Her heart gave an extra beat, then one more at the obvious tension in his voice. "Connor? Is something wrong?"

"No. Well, not yet, that is."

"What do you mean?" She gripped the receiver. "Where are you?"

"At the ranch."

This time her heart stopped dead. *Dooley messed up good today, caused an accident with my best cow pony so's I had to put the animal down. I was so gol-durned mad I lit into him, told him everyone would be better off it he'd just disappear.*

"Has there been an accident on Tanglewood?" she croaked, her throat sandpaper dry.

"No, no. I'm at the Bar G." He sighed. "It's Addie. I'm no expert, but it looks like she's in labor. How quickly can you get here?"

"I'm on my way," Lara said.

LARA DIDN'T BOTHER knocking at the back door, but entered the ranch house at the Bar

G. Connor met her at the foot of the staircase to the second floor.

"How's she doing?" she asked.

"She's havin' contractions pretty steady. In pain but managing." He actually rolled his eyes. "I'm pretty sure Addie's gonna do fine. It's Deke I'm more concerned about—"

"Lara!"

She glanced up to find the father-to-be standing at the top of the stairs looking as if he stared certain death in the face. His dark hair looked as if someone—namely himself—had been tearing at it madly, and the whites showed all around the irises of his green-gold eyes.

"God almighty, Connor," Deke barked. "What in hell are you doin', jaw-jacking with Lara while my wife's in mortal pain up here!"

"Obviously tryin' to make both your lives worse," Connor answered sardonically. "Once I have, my work here is done."

"Hello, Deke," Lara said calmly, climbing the stairs, Connor close behind her. Without a word, he indicated the door at the end of the hallway, then took Deke by the arm as he tried to follow her into the bedroom.

"What the hell?" Deke exclaimed, trying to shake off his friend's hold on him.

Connor only gripped his arm more tightly.

"Let's give the two women a moment alone, okay? Besides, I think we need to have a little talk about how to support one's wife when she's in labor."

"What? I swear, Brody, I'm this close to callin' you out—" Lara heard just before she closed the door behind her.

Addie Larrabie sat on the edge of a large four-poster, arms braced on either side of her as she bent over at the waist. She glanced up through a curtain of red hair.

"Oh, Lara! Thank heaven you're here. He was like to drive me crazy in the next minute!"

"You mean that wonderful husband of yours?" Lara asked, smiling. She set her medical bag on the mattress next to Addie.

"Wonderful?" She pushed her hair back impatiently. "Lord love him, he's been next door to worthless. For the first time in my life, I'm beginnin' to be glad he wasn't anywhere around for Jace's birth."

She flung another handful of her hair over her shoulder impatiently. "I swear, if it weren't for Connor, I doubt you'd be here. Deke dropped the phone three times trying to give you a call."

Lara spied a hair band on the nightstand and handed it to Addie, who gratefully gath-

ered her thick mane back and put it in a po-
nytail.

"Well, I'm here now, and there's nothing
to worry about," she assured her.

"Even out here in the middle of nowhere?"
Addie asked with touching uncertainty.

"Honestly?" Lara said. "Very little. It's
good you've given birth before. Second babies don't tend to be as difficult as the first.
What was your labor with Jace like?"

"Not bad, relatively. I'd say only a few
hours of hard labor. I did have Daddy take
Jace over to Opal's for the night. She's our
housekeeper. I didn't want him to be around
in case I do some hollering."

She actually seemed remarkably calm and
in control, considering. That was a good sign.

"Well, I've called for an ambulance, in
any case," Lara told her. "Even if it doesn't
make it before the baby comes, we'll want to
transport you and the little one to the hospital to make sure you're both in good shape.
Do you feel like walking around a little bit?
That sometimes helps."

Addie groaned but acquiesced. "All right."

She rose heavily, with Lara's help, and they
took a couple of tours around the large bedroom before a contraction hit. Lara quickly
got Addie to the bed, where she rode it out.

"Whoa. That was a good one," Addie gasped.

"I think that's enough walking for now." Lara helped her settle herself back on the pillows, then sat down beside her. "You're doing great. We'll keep timing the contractions, and once it seems you're getting close, we'll get the guys in here to help out—provided Connor's been able to calm Deke down."

"If anyone can, it's Connor." Addie blew a lock of hair out of her face, giving Lara a sidelong glance. "You know, Connor told me last week that he found out his daddy is responsible for driving yours away."

Lara felt her heart give another of those wickedly disconcerting skips, but she managed to keep her features placid. "He did?"

"Yes." She shifted heavily, trying to find a more comfortable position on the mattress. "He's devastated, Lara. I mean, he wasn't laid this low even by Mick telling him in front of half the county that he was no son of his, when Connor was only trying to do the right thing."

Lara closed her eyes in sheer empathy. "Mick did that to him? Why?"

"Of course. Connor wouldn't've told you." She sighed. "Mick had it out for Deke from the first. At one point he rigged a fence shared by the Bar G and Tanglewood, then deliberately injured his prize bull so that the animal charged through the fence right into the pasture where Deke, me and the boys were working with calves."

She gazed at Lara solemnly. "Jace was on the ground when the bull charged into the pasture. Deke almost got killed saving him."

Lara gasped. "I—I didn't know that. What a...a horrible thing to do." *What a horrible man,* she thought. Even worse than she had thought. "Poor Connor," she murmured.

"Lara, I'm not tellin' you this so's to paint an even worse picture of Mick Brody or to drum up sympathy for Connor," Addie continued. "I'm telling you because first, through it all, Connor stood up to his father and was even the one who turned Mick in when it became known to him his dad was responsible for the incident. It takes a rare kind of man to do that."

She massaged her swollen belly. "But I'm also tellin' you this because even with all that—with Mick trying to kill Deke, and succeeding in killing his father—neither Deke nor I hold that against Connor—because he's that rare kind of man."

Lara got Addie's message loud and clear. "I don't hold what his father did against him," she said a trifle defensively. "Truly. But you can see how that sort of incident isn't easily gotten over."

She fiddled with the edging on the comforter. "I sometimes think it can be—then I recall the countless nights I laid awake in my bed and listened to my mother sobbing."

She met Addie's gaze. "My father's leaving changed our lives. I'm not saying that Mick Brody is entirely to blame. Dad was…troubled before then. But when he got the job at Tanglewood, things really seemed better. I was only four, but I could *tell*."

"And so Connor has to pay for what someone else has done?" Addie asked gently.

Lara thought of what Connor had said about both of them needing to work on issues. "I'm paying, too, Addie," she whispered. "I'm paying, too."

The other woman's blue eyes were discerning—and compassionate. "Well, I guess all I've got to offer in consolation is that it ain't over till it's over. Who knows what might still happen one day? I know that from experience." Addie took her hand and squeezed it. "There's always hope, you know?"

Her heart aching, Lara could only nod.

The sudden sounds of a scuffle coming from the hallway beyond the bedroom door brought both their heads around. Lara heard a few choice curses, none anatomically possible, before Deke burst into the room, Connor a step behind him.

"Hello, honey," Addie said mildly. "Anything wrong?"

Deke jabbed his thumb over one shoulder. "Did you tell him to keep me outta here?"

Addie gingerly pushed herself up, pulling the covers up around her hips. "Yes."

"You did?" He looked thunderstruck. "Why, Addie?"

She shrugged. "You just seemed so nervous, Deke, and I thought it'd be easier on you if you didn't have to see me—"

"So I'm nervous!" he shouted. "But I'm damned well gonna be at my wife's side when she gives birth to my baby!"

His words echoed in the room. Addie's hands shook as she straightened the comforter with meticulous movements. That's when Lara remembered the story of how Deke had only returned to the Bar G a year or so ago, to discover Addie had borne his son.

And how, while one could forgive such a thing, it wasn't human nature to automatically forget.

Deke seemed to realize that point at the same moment everyone else did. He dropped to his knees beside Addie and pressed her hand between his two large ones. "I mean, hell, Addie, of course I'll be here for you. Especially when I wasn't there for the first one."

Addie's eyes filled with tears, and that's when Lara saw how scared she truly was. "Oh, Deke..."

Husband and wife gazed at each other with such adoration, Lara had to look away, partly to give them privacy, partly because the love between them was somehow so strong and sure and unchangeable.

Oh, to have that feeling, where the trust outweighed the doubts tenfold!

She glanced up and found Connor's gaze upon her, his brown eyes as inscrutable as ever.

"Wh-what about Connor?" Lara asked. "I mean, so far as staying in the room to help out."

Addie pinkened becomingly. "I love you, Connor, but you're *not* gonna have a front row seat when I give birth."

Connor's eyes met Lara's again, and she knew he'd perceived the situation. "I don't think you've got much choice, Addie," he said. "Deke needs to be at your side coaching you through this, which means someone needs to give Lara a hand on the, er, business end."

Addie blushed even harder, all the way to the roots of her flame-red hair. "Oh, all right!" she exclaimed. "I've got a feeling once the baby starts comin' in earnest I won't care if the whole of Texas is in the room."

It wasn't long before the contractions *were* coming in earnest. Lara sent Connor to gather supplies, such as clean towels and bedding, while she and Deke helped Addie change into a nightgown and draped her with a sheet.

"I should've moved you into Houston near the hospital months ago," Deke said as another contraction passed, his arm around Addie's shoulders.

She rested her head on his chest, using the brief respite to catch her breath. "Well, maybe the baby'd have been safer, but I'd definitely have gone crackers bein' away from you and the ranch."

"Oh, so now you can't get enough of me?" Deke joked, giving her a kiss on the temple.

Addie certainly couldn't, it seemed, as her labor progressed. Although it felt like hours, it was relatively soon when Lara could see the baby's head crowning.

"Connor, I'm going to need you to take the baby once it's born," she told him, handing him a pair of sterile gloves from her medical

kit. "I'll clear its airway and make sure it's not in distress, but then I need to tend to Addie. Have you held a baby before?"

"No, but I can do it," he said without a hint of uncertainty.

Lara smiled. Maybe she wasn't as glad for his presence as Addie was for Deke's, but it was close.

She bent as the next contraction came, exhorting Addie to bear down as she delivered the baby's head, then its shoulders, then finally its tiny torso and legs.

"It's a girl!" she crowed, holding the baby aloft.

Addie struggled to sit up. "Is she all right?"

"Hot dog!" Deke hooted. "A little girl!"

"She appears to be fine," Lara assured the new mother as she cleared the infant's airway and did an Apgar rating before handing the newborn to Connor. He reached out for the child awkwardly but readily.

"Just support her head with one hand and her bottom with the other," Lara instructed, pleased when he caught on immediately.

Their eyes met for the hundredth time, then slid away.

It was another ten minutes before Lara was able to ensure Addie would be fine. She

helped Connor wash the baby and wrap it in a blanket before handing her to the proud parents.

"Oh, you darling!" Addie said, her face transformed as she gazed down at her newborn daughter. Deke gave a short cough and took a covert swipe at his eyes.

Lara had to turn away or betray herself. Heaven knew she was happy for Addie and Deke. But the intimate scene only drove home how such happiness might never be hers. Hers and Connor's. She simply didn't see herself with any other man, not in that way.

"Excuse me," she said hurriedly. She made it to the small bathroom at the end of the hall before she let go with a dry sob, which she stifled as best she could. It wasn't fair!

"Lara?" a voice called from outside the bathroom.

Lara leaned her head against the door, gathering her energy and courage. Then she turned and opened it in one swift move.

Connor stood on the other side, looking devastatingly handsome with his dark hair damp and falling across his forehead, and his shirt open halfway, exposing his muscled chest.

"Connor, hi!" she said brightly. "I was just cleaning up—and giving the new parents

some privacy." To prove it, she crossed to the small sink and began scrubbing her hands under the flow of the faucet. "Th-thank you for your help with the birth," she added, her back to him. "I couldn't have done it without you."

"None of us could have done it without *you*, Lara —"

"Wasn't Deke a basket case?" she interrupted in a breathless rush, nearly dropping the soap in her nervousness. "I thought I might have to give him a sedative for a minute there."

At the feel of two large hands on her arms, she jerked her chin up and met Connor's gaze in the mirror.

"Lara—"

"Don't say it, Connor," she begged. "Please."

"I have to." His face was haggard. "I'm sick inside about this. About us."

Gently, she shrugged off his grip and reached for a towel, drying her hands briskly. "It won't be this way forever. Especially since I'm going back to Dallas to take a position at the clinic where I did my internship."

His face was stricken. "Aw, Lara, no—"

"That's right, I'm the one who's leaving, after accusing you of doing so." She gave a small laugh. "Guilty as charged."

"And I know I said I didn't care if you left, but I do," he said. "I just… Can't we work it out somehow?"

She'd thought her heart couldn't ache any more than it already did, but she'd been wrong.

Sadly, she turned to face him. "That's just the thing—how can we know for sure? Because…you seem to be searching right now. Searching for a place to belong, for an identity that's all yours and not your father's."

She hung the towel back on its rod, smoothing it unnecessarily. "And I'm searching, too. For ways to deal with those unresolved issues, as you so accurately pinpointed, with trust. Trusting men. Trusting you." She faced him squarely. "And I think the best way to deal with those issues is for each of us to tackle them on our own and not in the midst of a relationship."

"And you can't do that here? I mean, while you're still working and living here?" He ran an impatient hand through his hair.

"I could, but—"

"Or I could move back to the Dallas area, too, like I'd thought about," he interrupted. "Things might be better away from Bridgewater and all the bad memories, you know."

"They might." She was surprised at how

calm she sounded. "But I believe what will be best for me—and for you—is to put some distance between us. I...I won't be like my mother, Connor, forever yearning after a man who'll never be mine."

He stared at her hard and long, a war raging in those deep brown eyes of his.

"I won't let you do it, Lara," he said at last. "I won't be pushed away." And to prove it, he reached out for her, his fingers sliding around the back of her head, his other hand clasping her around the waist, as he lowered his chin to kiss her.

Lara had a split second to decide whether to reject his caress or accept it. And in that instant in time she discovered the exact nature of her heart. For she not only accepted his kiss, she returned it.

Her mouth was as hungry as his, her breathing as sharp and deep as they plunged into the deepest of kisses, as if into a bottomless spring. Lara clutched his collar in both fists as Connor's large hands spanned her rib cage, lifting her toward him.

Then with a groan he tore his mouth from hers. "I won't let you do it," he repeated raggedly, his breath ruffling the hair at her temple. "I won't let you leave."

"I have to, Connor," she whispered against his neck.

"No." He pulled back slightly to gaze into her eyes. "I meant that I'll leave instead. I'd considered it before, and it makes more sense for me to go than you. You've got family here you care about, and you're makin' real progress with the clinic, making real inroads with the townspeople." He gave a rueful laugh. "I don't think there's much chance of me doin' the same, and I should know when to throw in the towel. So I'll go, and you stay."

He looked so very determined. So very Brody. Did she really know him—deep down? What kind of man was he, really?

"It's not within your power to make that choice for me," she said with a catch in her voice.

His chin dropped, not in defeat so much as denial, and Lara feared she'd still have a struggle on her hands, one she simply wasn't up to. She was that close to giving in—still.

Then, with what seemed a superhuman effort for him, he nodded. "Then I hope you find the answers you seek, Lara," he said.

"Y-you, too, Connor," she said around the enormous lump lodged in her throat. "I hope you find the answers *you* seek."

"Well, I'm sure like my dad in that respect,

aren't I?" He gave another bleak laugh that chilled her to the bone. "'Cause I got nothin' but time to do that. Nothin' but time."

Chapter Ten

"Dad."

"Son."

Connor stared through the thick glass at the man who sat on the other side, and noted the features that were so like his own: the direct, deep-set eyes; the straight, proud nose. The uncompromising chin.

No doubt about it, Mick Brody was his father. And Connor was this man's son. But to say they had much in common beyond that had to be untrue. Connor knew it must be. Because while he loved Mick because he was his father, he had no connection beyond that with the flawed, arrogant, heartless man who sat before him.

That was Mick Brody. Not him. Still, Connor seemed doomed to carry the Brody stigma to his deathbed. And it had cost him the woman he loved.

"So," Mick barked, "what's goin' on at Tanglewood?"

Connor didn't speak. Refused to, his jaw set mulishly. He didn't trust himself not to lash out in unrestrained fury at the injustice of it. Finally, he managed to rasp, "The ranch is fine."

"And the breeding program?"

"It's up and going just dandy. The herd is in the pink of health, and the hands're as happy as dogs with two tails."

He lapsed into a moody silence, scowling at the scarred Formica counter in front of him.

"Well, it sounds to me like *somebody's* got a burr under his saddle," Mick observed drily.

Connor shrugged inculpably. "You can't mean me. 'Cause I'm gold, Dad. Not a care in the world."

Now Mick scowled—at him. "You gonna tell me what's got you more sour than a green apple and surly as an old hound dog with a sore paw?"

Again Connor clenched his jaw, the model of filial respect. And look where it had gotten him.

Oh, what the hell, he thought.

"You wanna know what's wrong? It's *you,* Dad," he burst out.

"Me?" His father was clearly taken aback. "What'd I do?"

Connor surged forward in his seat. "Damn it, how could you?"

"How could I what?" Mick flung up a hand, indicating the room. "Hell, I got someone watchin' me 24/7. What could I have possibly done?"

"All right, a better question might be what do people still not know that you've done?" Connor countered. "Like being downright cruel to innocent men like Dooley Dearborn, running him off when you knew he had a wife and little girl who depended upon him!"

His father actually blanched, which only made Connor's ire rocket skyward. "What *did* you do to him, Dad? At least with D. K. Larrabie, you believed you had a right to take offense when he skipped town with your fiancée, but what did Dooley ever do to you?"

Mick ran a hand through his hair, a hand Connor saw was shaking. "Why are you asking, Son?"

It sounded too much like a stall tactic. "Because I've fallen in love with his daughter, Lara," Connor said with cutting frankness. He had nothing to lose by being cautious; he himself had already endured the worst from his father. "But wouldn't you know it, it doesn't seem there's much chance of her ever trustin' me, at least not like a woman ought to trust the man she'll be spending her life with, on account of my father being the destruction of hers!"

Connor slammed his hand down on the Formica, drawing a hard look from the guard. "How could you, Dad? What kind of a man does that to another person? Do you know the heartache they've been through because of you? And do you have any idea the hell I'm goin' through now? Because the way things look, I'm never gonna be with the woman I love!"

He sat back forcefully, breathing hard, his ire as high as it had ever been in his life. And he'd have said it felt good to finally have it out with his father except it didn't. It felt lousy.

Because he knew he hadn't any right to come down on him so. Yes, Mick was Mick, with all his faults. And sure, his father had done Lara's family wrong, giving her a right not to trust him. But what if the real blame for their relationship going south actually lay in Connor himself, in his own faults, which had nothing to do with his father or his name?

It was his most secret fear, one he'd barely been able to consider, but knew he must now: that what had happened between Mick and

Dooley wasn't the only thing coming between their children. What if Lara's problem trusting him was solely due to Connor himself? Because he'd lately come to recognize some tendencies he wasn't really thrilled with, like the self-serving streak that had him doing good deeds all over town in a way that had fooled no one, including Lara.

Like wanting what he wanted when he wanted it—meaning Lara—and the rest of the world be damned.

Connor finally glanced up, to find Mick staring at him as if he were visually dissecting him.

"So...you really love this girl, Lara?" his father finally said.

Connor sighed. "Yes. I can't see myself with anyone else, ever. But then, what's the saying? Like father, like son. Who knows but maybe I'll end up trying to salve my loneliness by marrying some decent woman I won't ever have a chance of loving the way she deserves."

Mick just glared at him in the kind of tight-lipped silence Connor had learned meant his father was about to explode with anger himself. Well, he didn't care. Let it rip.

Finally, Mick growled, "So your old man

is nothing but a selfish SOB without a lick of charity in his soul?"

Connor just glared back at him without answering.

"You got a pen on ya?" Mick asked abruptly.

Connor blinked. "Why?" he asked suspiciously.

"Why d'ya think? For you to write with!"

Wondering what his father was up to, Connor reached into the inside pocket of his sport coat to take out a pen.

His father nodded curtly. "Fine. Now find yourself something to write on, even if it's the back of your hand."

He produced a folded piece of paper from another pocket. "Take this down," Mick ordered, rattling off a phone number and address in Reno, Nevada. Connor scribbled it down, more puzzled than ever.

"So who's at this address, Dad?" he asked warily.

His father eyed him coldly. "I ain't tellin' you, in case you don't end up contacting 'em. But if you do, just be prepared to find out the *real* truth about your father, 'cause that's where you'll find it."

Dropping his chin, Connor examined the piece of paper, a sickening feeling in the pit of his stomach. The real truth. Did he want to know what that was? Because it didn't seem as if the discovery had any chance of being good. Where Mick Brody was concerned, experience told him bad news was inevitably followed by worse news.

What should he do? He'd always prided himself on not being afraid to face the truth, either in himself or in others. But this was different. *He* was different, after what had happened with Lara. He understood more than ever the fear of trusting—fear of trusting oneself as much as others.

"Connor."

He lifted his head, and while his father still wore that hard, proud look that was signature Mick Brody, for the first time Connor saw a chink in armor he'd believed strong enough to deflect any blow. A sliver of a crack through which he detected…understanding. Regret. And perhaps even a little of the love and respect that had nothing to do with him being Mick Brody's son, and everything about him being his own man.

He rose, holding up the piece of paper. "I'll think about it."

"Fine. Just…let me know how it comes out, okay?"

Connor turned away without answering.

Once again he was on the horns of a dilemma, unsure he wanted to know what the truth was.

How could it be worse, though, than what he already knew: That right now there appeared to be little chance he would have a future with Lara Dearborn?

LARA PULLED INTO the driveway, momentarily cheered by the sight of the cozy glow of lights shining from the windows of her home. She was just as gladdened by the warm smells of pot roast and cinnamon baked apples that met her nose as she entered her kitchen.

Up to her wrists in soapy water at the sink, her mother glanced over her shoulder at her. "Hello, dear. Supper's just about ready."

"You're going to spoil me, Mom," Lara said, hanging her jacket and purse on the back of a chair and peeking into the oven. Both roast and apples were bubbling merrily. "I'm afraid it'll be back to frozen dinners and pudding cups when you return to Dallas."

"Well, that's not for a few more days, so we'll both just enjoy it." She rinsed the cutting board she'd been scrubbing, and propped it in the dish drain. "I miss cooking for you."

Lara kissed Pauline on the cheek. "I miss being cooked for."

It was the first time her mother had men-

tioned when she'd be heading home. Not that Lara wished her mother gone. Having her here, especially now, was like a balm to her aching heart. But she'd gotten the feeling that Pauline was waiting for the opportunity to say something, although she couldn't imagine what.

Well, didn't she herself have some news to tell her mother?

"Actually, Mom, we might have a chance to cook for each other more often very soon." She looked at her mother. "I—I'm leaving the clinic, as soon as a replacement is found, and moving back to Dallas."

Pauline slapped her soapy palms on her apron front in dismay. "But, Lara, why? You enjoy your work here so much! And you're just beginning to earn people's trust. You can't leave them hanging like that. It'll make the next person's job that much harder."

Lara dropped her gaze. Trust. Yes, that's what it always came down to, didn't it? Love couldn't grow without it.

"I'll make sure there's a smooth turnover," she said.

There was an uncomfortable pause. Then her mother asked softly, "Is it because of the Brody boy?"

Lara's chin came up. "You mean has Con-

nor acted unfairly to me or anything?" she asked with sudden defensiveness. "He's not his father, Mom. He's kind and honorable and t-true...." Swallowing with difficulty, she gripped the back of the chair so hard her knuckles whitened. "He's a good man, Mom."

"I didn't think he'd done anything wrong," Pauline protested mildly. She sighed, concentrating on drying her hands on a dish towel. "Lara, life's too short not to forgive and forget and go on," she said suddenly.

"Is that right?" Lara couldn't have said why, but she was suddenly angry. Angry at her mother. Angry at life. "Then why have you never gotten over Dad's leaving? I mean, it's obvious that you're still affected by that."

Her mother's gray eyes grew large with apprehension. "But I have forgiven him!"

"You've never remarried, never even had any kind of real relationship with a man after Dad left."

"Lara, you were only four, you couldn't know—"

"So I'm asking you now, Mom, what kind of future could I have with the son of the man who's responsible for that? Or what kind of future could I have, always fearing that the man I love might disappear one night and leave me as a-alone and empty inside..."

Lara pressed the back of one hand to her lips to stifle a sob of sheer panic at finally giving voice to her biggest fear. Of sheer misery, finally giving voice to her mother's heartache, which she'd spent her whole life watching.

Tears sprang to Pauline's eyes as well, and Lara reached out to her. "Mom, I'm sorry. I shouldn't have said that."

Pauline made no move to take Lara's hand. "No. No, you're right. It's not the only thing that's needed to be said, that's for certain. But you must believe me when I tell you, I...I was protecting you, dear, the best I knew how."

"Protecting me?" Lara shook her head. "From what?"

There was another weighty silence, in which it seemed to Lara a whole lifetime passed. What did her mother feel she had to protect her from knowing? "What, Mom?" she said more gently. "What were you protecting me from? Please."

Her mother's mouth worked, as if the words were there, already in her mouth, but she hadn't the motor skills to say them. Then Pauline murmured softly, "The story's not mine to tell, Lara. Even now, that's all I feel I can say."

It was on the tip of Lara's tongue to press

her, to not take no answer for an answer. She deserved to know the truth! But the timer on the stove dinged at that moment, and Pauline turned away. Lara watched, as pot holders in hand, she opened the oven door and removed the roast. "Time to eat. Would you set the table, dear, while I dish this up?"

So. The evasion would go on, Lara thought sadly. Of course, she could continue to press her mother until she got the answers she needed. But to what end? It wasn't as if the situation would magically change and all of a sudden the way to happiness would reveal itself. Life didn't work that way.

Feeling as if the weight of the world had lit on her shoulders, Lara did as her mother asked. What else could she do but go on with life as normally as possible, all the while believing any relationship between herself and the man she loved was as remote as ever?

WITH A SIGH, Lara closed the clinic's front door behind the last patient of the day. She gazed into the evening darkness beyond the window, where the wind whipped at the treetops and sent a stray tumbleweed skittering down the middle of the street as if in one of those spaghetti westerns. She half expected Clint Eastwood to come riding up Main Street.

Or someone else, come to save the town. But no one appeared out of the gloom.

Thanksgiving was just around the corner, celebrating a harvest that prepared everyone for the bleak winter months ahead.

How appropriate, she thought. It had felt lately as if her emotions had already gone into hibernation, needing to be well into a months-long slumber before the cold, bitter winter began to rage outside.

Of course, this was southern Texas. The winters were more apt to be mild affairs, where the worst that could be expected were a string of days in the high thirties and a good thunderstorm or two. Not much to hunker down for.

Shrugging, she turned away from the door and got on with the rest of her closing-up ritual by shutting off the front office computer and turning on the answering machine.

It was times like this when she fully realized how few days she had left at the clinic. She had called the physicians group she'd worked with in Dallas before coming to Bridgewater, and they were eager to have her come back, pending finding a replacement here for her. Then she'd called an agency that placed health care professionals in underserved areas as part of a tuition loan forgiveness program, and they told her they could get a P.A. there within the month.

Which meant that by the first of the year, she'd be back in Dallas, where she could begin to put the pieces of her life back together again. Life without Connor, at least for now—

She turned her head. Was someone banging on the front door?

Grasping her stethoscope around her neck, Lara hurried to the front of the clinic, wondering who needed her help. She pulled up the shade and found herself face-to-face with Connor.

"Let me in, Lara," she heard him say, his voice tense with excitement. "I've got something to tell you."

Fumbling with the lock, Lara opened the door, wondering what news could have brought him here, and in such a state. She didn't dare hope it could be good.

But oh, *he* looked good. She would never get over those deep-set brown eyes, those deep dimples like crescent moons that always marked his face, whether he smiled or frowned. That long, lean body that she ached to know intimately. Those strong arms...

His eyes were as thorough in their inventory of her. As hungry, making her even more convinced as to the wisdom of her decision. If she stayed, they would not be able to keep away from each other.

Lara cleared her throat. "C-Connor, what is it?"

He stepped inside, closing the door after him, and indicated the sofa in the waiting area. "You might want to sit down first."

Lara sat, wondering what he had to say that was so important she might lose her balance from the shock.

His intent became pretty obvious to her, though, when he knelt on one knee in front of her, taking her hand between his two large ones, his gaze utterly earnest.

Butterflies invaded her stomach in droves. Was he going to ask her to...to marry him? But why now?

And what would she say? Immediately, the answer rose up in her from that part of her that hadn't learned yet how to fear: *yes! Oh, yes!* Despite the problems between them, it could work out, for she loved him with all her heart, and she knew he loved her. It *would* work out!

"Connor—"

"Lara—"

They'd spoken simultaneously, and squeezing her fingers, Connor said, "Let me, please."

She nodded. "Go ahead."

"I don't know how to say this except just to say it, Lara." He drew in a breath. "I was on my way back from Houston earlier when I got a call from Griff on my cell phone."

His grip on her hand was painful in its intensity, radiating up her arm, all the way to her throat, making it constrict.

"And?" she asked breathlessly—but it wasn't in anticipation of the question she'd first believed he'd come here to ask. No, something besides love shone in Connor's eyes: compassion.

"It seems your father has shown up at Tanglewood," he said.

INSTANT NUMBNESS OVERTOOK Lara's body. She literally could not breathe.

"Wh-what?"

"Your dad, Dooley." Connor's voice, sounding as if it came from far away, was uncommonly gentle. "He's at Tanglewood, right now. Griff's there with him."

The numbness left her as swiftly as it came as a possibility fired through every nerve in Lara's body. "He didn't call Aunt Frannie, did he? And tell her?" she cried. "He didn't tell my mother!"

Connor shook his head. "No. Just me."

The joints of her fingers cracked, she gripped his hands so hard. "Are you sure?"

His brown gaze was steady. "Yes."

Relief barely had a chance to settle in her before she let go of his hands and rose abruptly, needing with the restlessness of a caged animal to move. And somehow, that's exactly what she felt like at that moment: wary, mistrustful, her every nerve on alert, ready to defend and protect herself at a second's warning.

Her father had come back! A vision of him, young and strong and tall, assaulted her mind's eye, as longing hit her with the force of a tornado, making tears sting her eyes. She'd always let herself believe her father was dead. It had been easier than contemplating the truth: that he was alive and hadn't returned to her mother and her.

But he wasn't dead. And he'd come back.

Why now, though? And why had he stayed away?

Reaching the front of the counter, Lara spun to face Connor again as another thought occurred to her. "Why would he go to your father's ranch?" she asked. "I mean, especially after what Mick did to him?"

The flicker of pain that crossed his features registered with her, but she hadn't the wherewithal then to feel regret. It *was* a matter of survival!

"He came there because I asked him to come back," Connor answered calmly. "A few weeks ago, I contacted him, using a number my dad had given me."

"You called him with a number *your* father gave you?" Her head spun with confusion. "Why did Mick have his phone number?"

Connor rose, his own posture somewhat wary. "I don't know the whole story, but apparently they were in contact with each other. Have been for the past ten years."

Lara could only stare at him in mystification. Her father was alive and well, and had been in contact for the past decade with the man who'd destroyed him? Why hadn't he at least sent some word to let her mother and Lara know he was all right?

But he'd chosen to stay in touch with Mick and not his wife. And not his daughter.

She pressed her fingertips to her temples at the sudden throbbing there. "I—I don't understand."

"You're not the only one. I don't know the whole story myself, only what I've told you I found out when I called your dad's place in Reno." Connor hesitated, then continued,

"Here's the main thing, Lara. He wants to see you."

Another shock wave of emotion slammed into her, this time indignation. "Not Mom? He doesn't want to see Mom?"

Connor's gaze slid away under her scrutiny. "He didn't say...."

She took two steps toward him, jabbing the air with her index finger. "Because she's the one who never gave up hope of him returning, never stopped loving him, even though he left!"

A new fear struck her. What kind of man would she find if she went out to the ranch? And whoever she found, should she tell her mother?

Given what she already knew—that Dooley had left on account of Mick Brody, and yet had been in contact with him and not his own wife and daughter—it didn't seem the outcome could be anything but painful, devastatingly so. She just couldn't see it unfolding any other way.

She stared at Connor. It was his fault. Oh, he should have left well enough alone!

"So." Lara crossed her arms. "Did you really think that by finding my dad you'd right yet another of Mick Brody's wrongs?" she asked pointedly.

Connor frowned. "That's not fair, Lara, and you know it."

"No, it's not fair—but that's what's so very Brody about it, this messing around with people's lives and happiness like some chess master!"

"I was not." His expression turned thunderous. "If anything, I was trying to exhaust every possibility I had so I wouldn't lose you for good!"

"And you thought by bringing my father back we'd all kiss and make up and the two of us could live happily ever after?"

"No!"

She took another step toward him, desperately fearless. "Because it doesn't work that way, Connor! The pain doesn't automatically disappear!" She flung out her arms, vaguely aware she was on the verge of hysteria. "The trust doesn't magically spring up between people!"

"I don't expect it to. And that's *not* why I called him!" He held out a hand in appeal. "Good grief, Lara, do you honestly think it was easy for me, contacting the man my father destroyed, knowing there was the possibility he would come back to Bridgewater?" The crescent dimples on either side of his mouth had never appeared so mirthless. "Just think about it. A handful of people know right now what happened to Dooley Dearborn twenty-some years ago. Now *everyone* will learn the story of yet another sin Dad committed, and this one about the worst yet."

Lara felt her own mouth set grimly. He had a point, but she was unwilling to grant him that.

He took advantage of her silence to continue with feeling, "And do you think I honestly believe this'll give both of us what we need to set our doubts about our relationship to rest?"

She hesitated, then shook her head shortly.

It seemed to provide him encouragement, for he closed the gap between them to take her wrist, tug it from where it was wedged in the crook of her elbow, and engulf her hand in his strong, warm one. "What I do believe is that you'll never have the kind of happiness you deserve until *something* is resolved about your dad, whether in your own heart or by coming to terms with him, which you've got the opportunity to do. Afterward, whether you tell your mom about him or not is up to you."

Tears stung at the back of Lara's eyes. "What if I find out...find out that he didn't love her?" she whispered, chin down.

"Or didn't love you?" Connor asked gently. "I can't believe that's the case. Your mother wouldn't continue to love him as she still does."

Lara blinked rapidly, her thoughts spinning madly. Yes, her mother still loved her father. She always would, no matter that she could never have the life with him she'd wanted— one where she could trust with a deep surety that whatever happened, the two of them would make it through, together.

Instead, Pauline Dearborn had spent the best years of her life pining over a man who couldn't give her what she needed. Who she would always have doubts about, no matter how much she loved him and he loved her.

All Lara knew was that *she* could not be like that. Not about her father—and not about Connor.

"You should have just left it, Connor," she made herself say, her voice rasping and harsh in her throat. "You shouldn't have called… him." She couldn't even say the words: *my father.*

"I thought the truth would be better than not knowing. I still do."

"Well, I don't agree." She withdrew her hand from his, stepping away from him. "And

I think you should go back to Tanglewood with that message."

She could tell she'd stunned him. "What are you saying, Lara?"

She tilted her chin up as if she had all the courage in the world. "I'm saying you made a mistake, bringing him here. So you'll need to tell him that I'm not prepared to see him, not right now, not in this way. I don't know if or when I will be. But it's got to be my choice."

His eyes appraised her, and she had a sense that he could see into her very soul. It wasn't a feeling she needed to have extended or repeated.

"You're only avoiding the inevitable," he said.

"If I am, don't you think I've earned that right?" She was back to hugging herself.

"The right to choose when to see your father? Maybe. But to keep your mother from having that choice? No," Connor said emphatically. "You'll never have earned that right."

Lara flew at him then, grabbing handfuls of his shirtfront in her fists. He didn't move a muscle in response. "Don't you dare tell my mother he's here! Tell me you won't, Connor!"

He stared down at her—and she knew that he saw into her soul and understood her as she'd never been understood in her life. "I won't. Think about it, though, Lara. You're doing what you've despised my father for, and have judged me for—playing with people's lives and happiness."

"This is different!"

"Is it? Keeping the truth from people, even if you think you're protecting them?" Gently, he extricated himself from her grasp and stood back. "You know, I may not be James Bond or Clint Eastwood in some shoot-'em-up movie where the end justifies the means. But I'm not the villain here, either. I'm just an ordinary man who's somewhere in between, and I've never been afraid to stand on my own two feet and be judged fairly for being that man. And if you're not able to do that, either with your father or me, then that's *your* problem, not mine."

She wondered where he got the composure to stoop to retrieve his hat from the sofa and set it on his head, for she knew Connor Brody well enough to recognize how angry he was at that moment.

"You're right about one thing, though, I'll tell you that," he added. "I'm through with tryin' to make amends for deeds I didn't do. Both Dooley and I will be out at the ranch if either Dearborn woman wants us."

With that, he turned on his heel and in two strides was at the door. This time it opened with ease—and shut with a mighty bang, leaving Lara alone.

Chapter Eleven

In a flash, Lara was four again, crouched at the top of the staircase listening to her mother's desperate plea for her father to stay, his appeal, as anguished, to be let go.

Dooley, I'm beggin' you. Just...stay a little longer, won't you? That couldn't hurt, could it?

Could it, Pauline? I already feel like a man half-dead inside, with the other half bein' eaten away bit by bit. You're right—how could that hurt any more than it already does?

Lara's feet felt as if they were nailed to the floor, and just as wooden. Her heart, on the other hand, was pumping like pistons on a locomotive.

Don't let him go! The cry surged up from the depths of her soul. *Don't let him leave, not like this!*

Yet it wasn't her father that inner voice cried for. It was Connor.

What would she say to him, though? How could she make him understand how frightened she was, terrified out of her mind? Terrified of losing the only man she'd ever loved. Terrified she hadn't the ability within her to make him stay.

She caught sight of her reflection in the darkened window. Her eyes were enormous, her mouth a thin, tight line. She looked so small, so insubstantial, so scared. And so much as her mother had looked when her husband had left all those years ago.

Lara bent her head, dropping her face into her open hands. But she could not block out the sight, or her pain.

She had to admit it. She'd never tried to track her father down because she hadn't wanted to know why he'd left. Hadn't wanted to deal with the man he was in reality rather than in her hazy, indistinct memory. Hadn't wanted to confront the feelings of knowing her mother continued to love and mourn a man who, had he really wanted to—had he really loved them—would have stayed, no matter what.

It struck Lara that the reason she herself had never looked for her father, not once, was to protect her mother from knowing for sure. And to protect herself from the truth.

Yet hadn't that been what Pauline had told her—that she'd been trying to protect Lara? From what?

What was the real truth? That her father had been primed to leave long before Mick Brody had pulled the trigger to propel him on his way? Or was there some other reason he'd left? Oh, how Lara wished she knew!

Yet hadn't Connor just shown her the way to that answer, to the truth, and she'd rejected it—and him?

She was shivering. Lara crossed to the plaid sofa on legs that felt wooden, and sank down on it, trying to get a grip on herself. How could she have done that to him? She'd flown at him like a harpy, accused him of awful things, pushed him away, maybe this time for good!

No. No, he'd said he would wait for her at Tanglewood. He was there if she wanted him. He and her father. So she hadn't lost Connor yet.

But she still could, if she didn't go to him. If she didn't go toward the truth, whatever it was, because the status quo most certainly would keep her from being with him.

This time she mustn't creep silently away from the anguish filtering up to her from the bottom of the stairs. She might find out what she'd done to lose her father—but if she didn't go to Tanglewood, she most certainly would lose Connor.

Lara rose. Sat back down again. She had no strength in her legs. Well, then, she'd have to get it from somewhere! Drawing in a deep breath, she planted her palms on either side of her and pushed herself up. She swayed briefly, found her balance again and took that first step, her whole body still feeling as limp as a popped balloon.

Then she took the next step, then the next, and soon she was out the door and running for her car. She flung open the door and slid behind the wheel, those opposing sensations of feebleness and fervor warring for domination in her body.

Because she still didn't know what she'd find at Tanglewood. She only knew she must take a page from Connor's book and pursue the truth, or she'd never have the happiness she so deserved—with him.

Tanglewood.

Lara had never feared it more. The white letters stood out like the epitaph on a gravestone, making her shiver as she drove beneath them. What lay at the end of that lane could provide that kind of lasting serenity—or could be as ruinously final.

She'd made it this far, however. She couldn't turn back now.

Lara pulled to a stop at the front door, where her courage took a sudden dip. What would she find inside? *Who* would she find inside? The father she remembered teaching her his special brand of creative cussing, or the man who'd found the prospect of staying with his wife and little girl too arduous an existence? It simply didn't seem to her that, whatever the outcome of this meeting, it would be good. For anyone.

She jumped as the large oak door swept open, and she found herself staring out her car window at Connor.

"You came," he said simply. Still, with those two words he somehow acknowledged the effort it had taken her to get here.

Yes, she had come—for him. And her father had come back—for her and her mother. There could be no other reason.

She wouldn't know for sure, though, unless she took that next step. And she could do it, with Connor at her side.

Opening the car door, Lara stepped out and took his outstretched hand.

HE'D WONDERED IF she would come. Hoped against hope she would, but feared with the deepest doubt that she would not.

Connor stared down into Lara's clear gray eyes and saw the same emotions. But she was here. They were both here, trying to find answers despite the fear.

He hoped against hope those answers would bring them closer rather than drive them further apart.

She followed him silently inside as Connor led the way to the great room at the back of the house. He stopped short of the entrance, however. Was arranging this meeting the wisest course, really? He would rather cut off his right arm than see Lara hurt. Would rather lose her. It had nothing to do with his own wants and needs, only her happiness.

He turned to face her. "Lara, maybe this isn't such a good idea after all—"

"Let me see him," she said calmly. "I need to see him."

His eyes stung. He loved her so much in that moment, yet feared for her more.

He stepped aside.

Connor watched her approach the man who stood on the other side of the room, his back turned to them as he gazed in contemplation

out the darkened window that reflected his
visage rather than revealed the view beyond.

"Dad?" Lara said.

Dooley Dearborn turned. "Hello, Lara."

Father and daughter stood staring at each
other for a long moment, and Connor tried to
take a mental step back and look at Dooley
from Lara's perspective.

He wasn't a tall man, just a shade over five-
nine, Connor guessed. His hair, blond like
Lara's, was thinning on top. His face was
ruddy but smooth, giving him the appearance
of a man who had finally gained inner peace,
although it had been hard-won.

He'd said little since arriving at Tanglewood that morning, other than to ask to see
Lara. He never mentioned Pauline.

Dooley cleared his throat, obviously over-
whelmed at seeing his daughter for the first
time in more than twenty years. The sound
acted like a catalyst, for Lara took a step toward her father, and he toward her.

Yet it wasn't to rush into each other's arms.

"Why?" she demanded abruptly, and in
that single word Connor heard all the disappointment of a four-year-old girl. "Why did
you let Mick Brody drive you away from us?
Why?"

Dooley paled. "But, darlin'…Mick didn't

drive me away. Not a'tall. Why would you think that?"

Connor stifled a gasp of surprise. Lara's, however, was audible—and incensed. "I heard him tell Mom the night you didn't come home. He said you'd messed up at the ranch and he was so mad he ran you out of town."

"And you've believed that, all these years?"

Lara's mouth trembled, but she answered firmly. "Yes." Her gaze faltered then. "I don't think Mom ever has, not completely. But I think she pretended to believe it, for my sake."

The older man lowered his chin with a shake of his head. "Aw, Mick, you big..." He sighed, lifting his head, and there were tears in his eyes. "He must have staged that scene to help me save face with you and your mother, should I ever want to come back. But that's not what happened at all."

He started toward her, yet something in her expression stopped him. "I left because I wanted to leave," he said gently. "I couldn't handle life with you and your mom the way it was, and I had to get out."

Connor's heart twisted in his chest. It was exactly what Lara had most feared. Exactly.

Her knees seemed to buckle beneath her, and instantly Connor was at her side, helping her to perch on the edge of the leather sofa.

He sat beside her and, unable to stop himself, engulfed her small hand in his larger one.

Her dazed gaze slid away from her father and focused on him, and Connor had never seen someone look so devastated—except, of course, for himself. He'd glimpsed that same expression in his own eyes too many times, especially in the past year.

Yes, he would have given anything to spare her this ordeal, but since he couldn't, he would be with her every step of the way.

She must have seen something in his gaze that helped her, for she turned back to her father. "M-maybe you'd better tell me what happened."

Dooley himself seemed unsteady on his legs, for he sank into an armchair opposite. Still, he seemed willing—even determined— to tell his story. To tell the truth.

"I guess I should start at the beginning," he finally said after two false starts. "About how I came back from Nam a shell-shocked twenty-one-year-old without the ability to grasp what I'd experienced there, much less heal myself from it."

He leaned forward, forearms resting on his knees, hands clasped between them. "I think things would've been manageable, but the 'war' here was almost as bad. Along with thousands of other vets, I was gettin' attacked daily in the newspaper and on TV. I even had a woman spit on my shoes as I got off the plane from Honolulu."

At that, Lara made a small sound, almost of empathy. But she didn't interrupt Dooley as he went on musingly, "It was like I'd sacrificed everything, and it was for nothing. So I did the only thing I could think of, and tried to put it behind me, tried to live a normal life by getting married and having a daughter…."

He met her gaze squarely. "You. You were…the best thing that ever happened to me, Lara. You've got to believe that."

Connor felt Lara's grip tighten on his. She said not a word.

Nodding, Dooley took her silence in stride. "The problem was, the…the depression I came back from Nam with never went away, not completely. It was always there, like my memories of the war, in the back of my mind, just sort of bubbling there, waiting to come to a boil."

He rose abruptly, obviously at the toughest part of his story, and took half a dozen steps away from them, his hands thrust in the pockets of his slacks as he stared again out the window—at what, Connor didn't know. It was pitch-black out there, making the smooth glass a mirror again reflecting Dooley's face.

"I did anything I could think of to forget," he continued, still turned away from them, although they could see his somber expression clearly in the window's reflection. "You and your mother helped me do that...most of the time. But I have to admit it—sometimes knowing you loved me and depended upon me made it worse. When I took the job at Tanglewood, I can see now that I was probably on the edge of a breakdown."

He shot Connor a glance over his shoulder. "Your father saw that somehow, you know."

Now Connor's worst fears crowded forward. Still, he made himself ask, "And what did he do?"

"Well, it wasn't anything big, not in the scheme of things," Dooley answered. "Mostly, he'd find opportunities to ask me about my experiences overseas. I could tell nothing I said could shock him, not even the worst of my feelings. And it made things better for me. Easier. Mick even turned a blind eye to my showing up late or cutting out early without a word when flashbacks came upon me. Then one day—" He broke off, his jaw working.

"What happened, Dad?" Lara asked softly. Her support seemed the one thing he needed to get through this, for Dooley continued resolutely, "One day when I and the other hands were out moving cattle, I was chasin' one rogue steer along the riverbed. The mare I was ridin' hit a hole and we went tumbling down the bank into a ravine. I was shook up—but Sassafras broke a leg. Mick had to destroy her then and there, and when that gunshot sounded, everything came rushing in on me, like I was there again."

There—in Vietnam. *It must have been a horror,* Connor thought.

"I'm ashamed to say I lit out for the highway then and there," Dooley admitted quietly. "Mick caught up with me and tried to talk me into staying, if not for myself, then for my wife and little girl. But I was convinced you'd be better off without me."

He shrugged, a simple lift of his shoulder. "So I left. Left you and your mother."

"That's what Mick was doing at our house that night," Lara said dazedly. "He wanted to convince Mom that he was responsible for your leaving." She stared at Connor. "And I blamed Mick all these years for something he didn't do. He was trying to keep me from blaming my father. Oh, Connor, can you forgive me?"

It never occurred to him to answer any differently than to say, "There's nothing to forgive, Lara. Honestly. I mean, it's obvious that was what Dad wanted you to think."

He could tell she wasn't about to believe it was that simple.

"I hope you'll find a way to give Connor— and Mick—that forgiveness, hon," Dooley murmured. "As for me, I can make explanations, but I won't give you excuses," he told her with solemn gravity. "I sure enough went through a bad spell of livin' on the rails, livin' on the streets. Somehow I ended up in Reno, God knows why. But I was able to get my life together with the help of the local V.A. office. Now I'm doin' that for other vets down on their luck. I've come to see that it's not just the way things happened, it's the way they were meant to be. Helping those men is why I'm here on this earth. And while I don't dare hope that you can forgive *me* for walkin' out on you and your mother, I'm hoping you'll understand why I did."

He took a deep breath, apparently needing to say one more thing. "Mick caught up with me in Reno ten years ago—and he tried to convince me again to come back to Texas. To come back to you, Lara, and your mama. But even though I was better, I didn't feel it was right to barge back into your lives. And you were doin' fine, too. Mick would occasionally check up on you through some acquaintances he had in Dallas, and would let me know. Every six months or so I'd get a letter from him with some bit of information on you—what you were doing and all."

"And he never told you what he told Mom that night you left?" Lara asked.

"Not other than he explained the situation to her. He didn't say how, and I didn't have the nerve to ask."

Silence fell in the room. The measured tick of the clock on the fireplace mantel struck an incongruent counterpoint to the wind whistling and moaning outside.

Then, of a sudden, Lara stood. Dooley swung around, fists still crammed into his pockets. With obvious purpose, she walked toward her father. His eyes flared open momentarily, but other than that, he didn't move, didn't shy away, even as his daughter stopped in front of him, emotion radiating from her slight figure.

"I'm glad to finally know the truth, Dad," she said. "Not that it makes the pain go away. But it helps make things make sense—things I never understood. Or understood but didn't want to face."

She reached out and, tugging his hand from

his pocket, took it in hers. Dooley's face was a study in yearning at that first contact with his daughter in two decades. "And I know you don't expect me to forgive you, but I do, Daddy."

Her voice broke. "I—I don't want to hold on to those old hurts any longer than I have to. I want to be happy."

"You will be, darlin'," her father whispered. His eyes met Connor's over the top of her head in a silent question. Connor nodded soberly. "You will be. That I can promise you."

His hand visibly shaking, Dooley lifted it to tenderly brush back a strand of that wheat-colored hair. And when Lara bent her head to lay her cheek against his palm, Connor had never been so glad. The best deed he'd ever done was bring Dooley Dearborn home.

They all started as a ferocious pounding started on the front door of the house.

"Someone's here," Connor said inanely, but before he could answer the door, in rushed Pauline Dearborn.

She stopped dead in the middle of the room, her hair flying in ten different directions. Her gray eyes were huge in her face as she stared at her long-lost husband as if he were an apparition.

"Hello, Pauline," he said.

"Griff told me you were here," she gasped, as if she'd run every step of the way to Tanglewood. "I know you didn't ask to see me, not yet, but I had to come, Doo. I had to."

Dooley drew himself up with dignity as Lara stepped away from him. "I'm not here to stay, Pauline."

"You...you're not?" she choked out, her hand fluttering at her throat.

"No. I've only come to set aright the wrong I did to you and Lara here those years ago— as best a person can that sort of thing. I know it doesn't take away the pain you've suffered."

He gestured toward his daughter. "I've been explaining to Lara what happened. Apparently, Mick Brody told you some fiction about runnin' me off, which isn't true. I'd like the chance, if you'll let me, to give you the real story, Pauline. Then I'll go."

"No," she said.

Dooley blinked. "No?"

"No, I won't let you, either explain or leave again." Pauline crossed the room, and this time Connor thought Dooley would actually give in to impulse and back away.

He didn't, though, not even when Pauline grasped both his hands in hers. "I don't understand, Pauline."

"Oh, don't you see?" she cried. "It doesn't

matter what happened. Why you left, which I know, Doo. I've always known. That and why you stayed away. And now why you've come back."

She put her arms around him. "All I care about is that you're here."

Dooley stiffened. "And...you'll forgive me?" he asked in disbelief.

"You're already forgiven. From the moment you left, you were."

With a groan he crushed her to him. Then, catching sight of their daughter, Dooley extended an arm toward her, and she went into the circle of her parents' embrace.

Pauline gave her daughter an especially fervent squeeze. "But will you forgive me, Lara?" she asked.

Lara shook her head in confusion. "Forgive you, Mom? For what?"

"I always suspected that Mick had made up that story about driving your daddy away. I knew how... troubled Dooley was by what he'd been through in the war, and I knew Mick was one person who understood that. So I let him play out that scene about driving your daddy away—and I let it go on as you grew up because I thought it best for you to believe that instead of knowing the truth."

"Was it because you thought I'd want to go find Dad if I knew the truth?"

"Yes—and bein' with us, his family, wasn't where he needed to be." She turned back to her husband, her expression one of infinite gentleness. "I never gave up hope that he'd return when he was able. Never stopped loving him, either. For that's how love is, you know."

She took Dooley's face between her hands. "Love already knows the truth in your heart. It's finding a way to believe what your heart tells you that's hard for some of us, sometimes. In the end, though, the truth comes out—and it sets you free."

Connor's eyes blurred with unshed tears. He had never heard truer words in his life. Out of the corner of his eye, he saw Lara blink back tears that had come to her own eyes.

"Hell's bells and little antlers." Dooley's blue eyes filled with tears, too, as he gazed at his wife. "I love you, Pauline," he said roughly, pulling her close again as her eyes drifted closed in pure contentment.

Connor touched Lara's elbow. "Come on. I think your parents could use a minute by themselves." He took her hand. "And I could sure use a minute with you."

"Wait," Dooley said. He peered at Connor. "So Mick's in prison at Huntsville?"

"Yes. He murdered a man, and almost killed his son."

Dooley's mouth thinned in regret. "I'm sorry for that, Son. I truly am. There's no disputing that he must pay for his crimes, but there is redemption in Mick Brody, make no mistake about that. It's been your daddy's continued support and friendship that brought me here today."

Unable to speak, Connor nodded. Turning back to Lara, he found that her eyes were shining with happiness—for him. For what this moment of truth meant to him, too.

They said nothing, but walked side by side out to the patio at the back of the house. Under the arbor, he turned toward her and captured her in his arms as he'd wanted to do for weeks. Captured her lips as he'd been dying to do for a lifetime.

Lara's response was to cleave to him, wrapping her arms around his neck and whimpering with a need that satisfied him to his toes. God, he loved her, would like nothing more than to never let her go again. But they had some unfinished business between them.

He lifted his head. "Look, Lara. We've got a long way to go to get our relationship on solid footing, you know. I'm confident we'll make it, but I can do only so much to bring you to that belief—"

He was cut off by the kiss she planted on his mouth. Heavens, she had the lips of an angel, full and tender and all-giving. Then she slid her hands inside his jacket to tug his shirt from his jeans in a way that was most *un*-angelic. Connor sucked in his breath when her small hands slid up his back, raising goose bumps the whole way, the sensation of her touch on his skin was so electric.

And he couldn't help himself. He'd held back for so long, tried to banish all hope of ever holding her again.... He pulled her deeper into the shadow of the arbor. There, he let himself go, kissing Lara as if she were his sustenance.

He needed to touch her, too, and even though the cool November night had fallen in earnest, he didn't hesitate to quest inside the warm recesses of her coat. He pulled her own shirt from her slacks and stroked his fingertips up the side of her rib cage to her breast, making her moan with pleasure, to his great satisfaction. In fact, when she pressed into his palm, it made him want to disregard everything he'd just said and had yet to say, and make love to her here. Now.

He couldn't, though. "Lara, wait, I have something to tell you," he mumbled against her lips, resisting—albeit not very hard—the tug of fingers on his wrist as he tried to draw his hand away. "Lara—"

"Relax, Connor," she murmured.

"I can't relax! This is too damn important, important to us."

She sighed. "All right. Tell me what's on your mind."

He gazed at her earnestly. "I've got to know, Lara. Are you going to be able to love me not because of what I've done to make up for my father's wrongs or because I've brought your father back into your life, and not in spite of what I've overcome as a Brody, but for *me?* Because that's what I need from you. I won't take anything less."

Lara smiled. "Well, I'll certainly give it my best shot."

"Your *best shot?*" he echoed, incredulous at her nonchalance.

"Of course. I mean, you said it before, that trust isn't built in a day. So I'll try my best to work toward trusting you for yourself and not because of any issues I have with your dad or mine."

"Well…all right then," Connor blustered, uncertain whether he'd just painted himself into a corner or not as he looped his arms around her waist and she snuggled into him again.

"Uh, just to let you know, though," she added, "I'm like my mother."

"Meaning?"

"Meaning that I already love you, and nothing you are or do can change that."

Tenderly, she took his face between her hands, just as her mother had done with her father. "Of course, I love you even more dearly for restoring my dad to me and my mother. But I fell in love with you for the extraordinary man you are. For never giving up, never shying away from the truth, even when it might have brought you more pain at your father's hand and pushed us further apart."

He swallowed past the lump that suddenly sprang to his throat. "I'm not extraordinary," he said modestly. "Not at all. But for once I am proud to call myself a Brody."

Then he tugged her close again. "And I hope you'll do me the honor someday of calling yourself a Brody, too."

"Oh, with pleasure," Lara sighed as he bent once more to kiss her. "With the greatest pleasure in the world."

* * * * *